QUEEN OF DREAMS

A DARK RH ROMANCE PETER PAN RETELLING

BRUTAL NEVER BOYS 3

MONA BLACK

QUEEN OF DREAMS
(BRUTAL NEVER BOYS #3)

What makes us go back to our fears and dark desires, again and again, unable to escape?

I thought it was all over. That I was back in the human world, for good this time. Back in my apartment, with my friends, my job, my life.

But the heart works in mysterious ways and it won't let me rest. When I find out that the Lost Boys might still be alive, I jump at the chance to go back to the island and save them.

Losing them would be unbearable, even though I ran away from them once before.

Only problem is, saving them means I'll have to face my greatest fear, plunge into the unknown and accept what I did and who I am.

Can I do it?

Will it work?

And even if I manage... where do we go from there? Will love prove strong enough to save us all?

NOTE: this is the third and final book in a trilogy featuring mature situations with some dark themes and adult language. Warning for DubCon, blood, gun, & Knife play, violence, kidnapping, stalking, forced proximity, bondage, light bdsm, unhinged psycho men and M/M relationships.

PART I

"To die will be an awfully big adventure."
— J.M. Barrie, Peter Pan

1

WENDY

"Jas," I whisper, running down the stairs and stepping out, onto the street. "It's you. Jas!"

Cold wind hits me, sending me a step back. I lower my head against it. He's still there, staring at me with wide eyes, his dirty white shirt flapping a little, his black slacks looking kind of torn and rumpled.

Holy crap. It really is him.

"Wendy," he breathes. "You know me?"

"I remember you. You were on the island."

"You do remember it, then." His jaw relaxes a fraction, then tightens again. There is a ticking sound. He's gripping a pocket watch in one hand. It seems to be encased in crocodile skin. "That's not good."

"Why not?"

"You were supposed to forget. Always forget, whenever you come back home. It's how it works."

"Well, I do remember you, and... Peter and the others."

He's frowning but even so his gray eyes widen a little. "God almighty."

Such a quaint little swearword, so fitting with his clothes and bearing, and yet...

A savage grin, a bruising grip, a violent thrust between my legs, a snarling shadow at his back—

"Wendy." He catches my hand as I gasp for breath, trying to sort through swirling memories of faces, places, moments, recent and old, buried and foggy, bright and sharp.

"Let go."

"Fuck, sorry." He releases me, mouth tightening. "I shouldn't have come here. I just wanted..."

"What?" I clasp my hands together, press them to my churning stomach. "What did you want?"

"To see that you're okay," he says.

"Why wouldn't I be?"

"Because your memories of your past had returned, dark memories, so I thought..." He sighs. "Fuck, it was stupid. You probably forgot all about that already."

I shake my head. "I haven't."

Another gust of wind makes my teeth chatter.

"Damn," he says. His face is burned by the cold, his lips chapped, his eyes red-rimmed. He has streaks of what looks like dried blood on his bare forearms, under his rolled-up sleeves.

He has to be freezing his ass off in this weather.

So I make a strategic decision. "Come on up."

He blinks, pale lashes sweeping back up, bright eyes boring into mine. "Not a good idea."

"You'll get hypothermia if you stay out here dressed like this. That wouldn't be a good idea, either. Where's your coat?"

"Didn't bring my garderobe with me, sweet cheeks."

"Garderobe?" I blink. "You mean your clothes? Left them on the island?"

"There isn't an island to speak of, Wendy, if you recall," he says quietly. "It has sunk to the bottom of the ocean."

Swallowing hard, I nod. "Yeah, I know."

"There's only a rock left out of the waves, what used to be the Hill, so I had to cross over here to... to get provisions."

He sounds like he wanted to say something else. I grab his hand and he jerks a little, obviously not expecting it.

"Come on up. We can talk there."

"About what?" He doesn't resist, though, letting him tug him inside the building and up the stairs. "It's over."

"You're still alive, though. How?"

"I was on that rock." He sucks a sharp breath. "Last man standing."

Opening the apartment door, I lead him inside and shiver pleasantly at the warmth instantly enveloping us. "And what did you do? I thought... I thought you would jump into the sea, too."

"What do you care?" He pulls his hand free, examines it as if I wounded him just by holding it. "You're home now."

I open my mouth to retort something, but I'm not sure what it would be. So instead, I open the kitchen cupboards. "I'll make us some tea."

"You don't..." He hesitates. "Ah, fuck it. Got anything stronger?"

I turn to look at him. His handsome face is drawn and his hands are shaking.

"Sit," I say, pointing at the small table. "Vodka okay?"

"Whatever you have," he rumbles, sitting down with a grunt.

I open the cupboard below the sink and take out a bottle. "Charlie likes it. She's my roommate. She's—"

"Right here. She's right here." Charlie appears from her bedroom, arms folded over her breasts, one brow lifted. "Dee, for Christ's sake, what are you doing?"

"What?" I'm still holding the bottle of vodka. I place it on the table. "What does it look like I'm doing?"

"Wendy Persephone Darling," she says, exasperation in her voice, "will you finally stop bringing strangers up to our apartment? What's up with you?"

"He isn't a stranger," I protest, waving a hand at him. "I know him."

She glares. "From where?"

Settling his blood-streaked arms on the table, Jas gives Charlie a flat stare, not making any movement to get up. He looks like he's too tired to give a damn. Or maybe he just doesn't care.

I can still see the monstrous shadow arching over him. So much like Peter's shadow, though Peter's is human if corrupted, and his... his isn't human at all.

"From before," I say vaguely and turn back around to take three small glasses. "Vodka?"

"No, thanks." She scowls. "Not going to drink with this random guy you picked up on the street. Is this how it's gonna be from now on? Should I start looking for another place to live?"

"Charlie." I put the glasses down on the counter, my heart starting a sick pounding. "Are you serious?"

"Are *you*? You can't bring up every man you find on the street, Dee, even if they're... handsome and all." She waves a hand at Jas. "You don't know them."

"I just said I do. From... a party. Recently."

"A party." That skeptical eyebrow goes back up. "Really."

"Really! Now, will you sit?"

"Nah, I'm going to bed. I'm tired and I work tomorrow, just..." Finally, she looks at me, her eyes pleading. "Be careful, Dee. I mean it. You're so trusting sometimes, I swear, and there's so much evil in the world."

"I know that," I whisper as she turns around to go. I hear the lock turn on her bedroom door. "I know."

I don't think she hears me.

But Jas nods at me, as if we're agreeing on something. "How about that drink?"

"Coming right up," I mutter, grabbing two of the glasses and sitting across from him.

Like a déjà vu from less than ten minutes ago when I sat here with Charlie, but now it's as if my world not only has been turned upside down but is firmly rooted in this absurd position.

In this absolute madness.

Across from me is sitting a man from Neverland, the Captain of the ghostly pirates, the one with the crazy alien shadow who bound me and fucked me into the ground, then saved me by sending me back here and...

"And what now?" I whisper the question that has been underlying my every thought since my return.

"Now?" He watches as I grab the bottle and pour Vodka into both glasses—then he takes both and empties them, one after the other, down his throat. "More."

Without a comment, I pour again but snag one of the glasses for myself before he finishes them, too.

He tosses the Vodka down his throat and thumps the glass on the table. Licks his lips. Nods again. Glances around. "So... This world has changed a lot since I was last here."

"Which was when?" The Vodka burns going down, even if I'm taking small sips.

"Oh, you know. A few centuries, give or take. Peter... he updated me on language changes. And technology and stuff." He shrugs his big shoulders. Sweeps his pale hair off his face. "Kept me updated until... until our falling-out."

"Is that what you're calling it now?"

A sigh is my only answer. He grabs the bottle and pours himself another drink.

"And I didn't know you could hop between worlds." I swirl the Vodka in my glass. "I thought only Peter had that ability."

"It has long been believed that only one of us could travel. The one who'd accept the title of the king, and that was Peter."

"He said it was forced on him," I muse.

"It was. In a manner of speaking."

I knock back the rest of my Vodka and wince. "You like riddles. So Peter could hop between worlds while he was king and now...?"

"Now he's dead," Jas says, voice harsh and brittle, and this time he drinks directly from the bottle.

Oh boy, Charlie won't like that. Better not tell her.

Then again, we're about to finish the bottle. I'll buy her a new one. I'll buy her two, I'll...

Stop avoiding the pain, I tell myself. *Face your memories. Face your fears. You owe it to Peter and the Lost Boys, at least.*

And God, it hurts.

"I can't believe he's dead," I whisper, and my voice cracks right through. "That they are all dead. This is my fault."

"Wendy..." Unexpectedly, he takes my hand—and this time, I let him, grateful for the pressure of his long fingers over mine, his rough palm, his solid presence. This sharing of the sorrow.

"I'm so sorry." My breath hitches. "So very sorry. I'm—"

A flash of darkness blinds me—of pain and fear and despair, taking away my senses so that I'm drowning, dying. Gasping for breath, fighting for the next heartbeat. Sinking into the void, with snapping fanged mouths and clawed hands and—

"Wendy? Are you okay?" I blink and find Jas leaning over me, over the table, giving me a concerned look. "What is it?"

One thing is clear in my mind. Despite the similarities with my nightmares, what just hit me is not a memory.

It's *them*.

"It's Peter," I whisper. "He's alive." I swallow hard. "They all are."

I have to go back.

2

WENDY

"They are alive?" Jas straightens, pale brows drawn together in a frown. "No, no fucking way. I never thought... Fuck, the merfolk."

"Is it possible?" I breathe, still reeling from the vision—was it a vision? "I could swear I was right there, in the sea, but I'm not wet, so I wasn't, and—"

"Oh, it's possible. That you were there, that they're alive." He gives a dry bark of laughter, though his face is now carved in strange lines of hope and pain. "I just never thought the mermaids would take such a risk and let the undying live."

"Undying?" I squeak. "You just said you thought they'd been killed."

"There are ways to kill the unkillable, if you know what I mean."

"I don't. Jas—"

"The reason you aren't wet is the portal between the worlds," he says, frowning at the bottle in his hand. "The time displacement and the magic in between. And it doesn't matter whether they are dead or alive if the mermaids have them."

He tips the bottle up, catching the last drops on his tongue and I swallow hard, annoyed with myself because in spite of the onslaught of memories, the pain and fear they bring, the stabbing panic at the impossibility of it all, I can't help but watch and want this man.

Wanting him to use his tongue on me, to grab my wrists and hold me in place, take me rough and hard, as he'd done on the island—

"Wait." I lift a finger. "Wait... What do you mean it doesn't matter if they are dead or alive? It's all that matters! We can get them out of there! Set them free."

"And then what? Neverland is gone. Neverland was never meant to last. It was made of your nightmares and fears."

"Why?" I whisper.

"I thought Peter would have explained it to you."

"I'm nobody special. But Peter... Peter saved me. When I was a kid. Pulled me out of the sea, saved me from drowning. I owe him, if nothing else. I have to save him. Save them all."

"So it's a matter of owing him?" he asks.

I shrug, avoid his gaze.

"Anyway, you can't," he says harshly. "It's done."

"Says who? Your Fae master? What does he have over you? They are alive, Jas, we can get them out!"

"I don't have a master. I was only trying to stop the idiots from meeting this fate but they fell for you." His voice cracks. "Which..."

"Which?"

"Fuck." He shoves back the chair and jumps to his feet, turns to go. "Which is why I came here. Don't know why?"

I shake my head. "You need my help to set them free."

"I didn't even know they lived when I came, though I should have felt them, but I'm blinded by what I feel, by—"

"What you feel? What do you mean?"

"It's you," he snarls, his handsome face suddenly twisting

and I don't know if it's rage or sorrow or something else entirely.

"Me?"

"It's... different with you. Peter and the Lost Boys... are everything to me. Everything, do you understand? My family, my friends, my lovers. Or they used to be. But those feelings never changed. I changed sides to save them, and I failed, but they hated me for it and I still want them. But then you show up... changing the game. What I feel for them is sharp, for you it's gentle, for them it's bittersweet, for you it's earthy, for them it's violent, for you it's... well."

"I'd say it's violent, too."

A shadow of a grin teases his full mouth.

"What are you trying to say, Jas?"

"That I came here to see you. See if you're okay. I never thought you'd want to go back. That you'd be in love with them, too."

"We have that in common, huh?"

He laughs. "I suppose we do. And what about me? Do you love me, too?"

"Still trying to figure that one out," I mutter.

"Fair enough." He's still grinning, and despite the thinness of his face, the obvious fatigue, he looks so beautiful it burns.

I whisper, "If Peter is still alive... still the king... how do you explain that you were able to travel here?"

"I never said I wasn't. The bridge is still standing, you see. The bridge between reality and dreams, the bridge that threatens to destroy the world."

"But—"

"To travel, you need a Fae token. It helps you focus. The King of Neverland gets a magical acorn." His gaze dips to my collarbone where the golden acorn is resting. "That allows him to slip between worlds."

"But he gave it to me and still he traveled here last time."

"And you gave him a silver thimble. As for me... Look." He takes his crocodile-skin pocket watch out. "Still ticking."

"It's cracked."

"Because I threw it into the sea, thinking it was all over. The mermaids brought it back to me. What matters is that it's still working. It will only stop when the bridge has fallen. My magical Fae token. My curse and my power."

I shake my head. "This makes no sense. You never traveled between worlds before."

"I did. I tried to stop Peter from taking you the first time."

I flinch. "That was you? The man who attacked me before Peter grabbed me?"

He nods. "I'd apologize, but I was trying to save you. Save all of them. And yet, all I managed was to make them hate me. Peter... He'd never believe that all I wanted was to save him."

"You stabbed him once."

"And he stabbed *me*. That was long ago, though. Listen, Wendy... You can go back, but that doesn't mean you can save them. Chances are, you'll die. And I... fuck, I don't want you to die."

I cock my head to the side. The alcohol has made me dizzy —or maybe it's him. His presence, his scent, his voice, his admission.

This weird discussion that nevertheless makes more sense than anything else in my life right now.

"I said it," he whispers. His gray eyes glimmer. "Can't take it back."

"I don't want you to take it back," I make my own admission. "But I'm still going."

"I knew it was a mistake to come here."

"And yet you came."

"I keep making mistakes," he whispers. "I should have stopped you from leaving this world the first time. I should have seen it, seen what would happen. I shouldn't have gone there in the first place. I shouldn't have come here."

"I'm glad you did."

"Are you?" He walks around the table, pulls me to my feet, hauls me against his tall, hard body.

It takes my breath away.

I splay my hands on his broad chest, breathe him in, dark spice and masculine sweat and sex—and meet his gaze without flinching.

"Yes, Jas. I am. I'll save them. Save all of you."

"And if you can't?" he asks softly.

"Then at least I'll have tried."

"And then what? Bring us all to live here?"

"Is it so bad here?"

"No, it isn't." He sighs. "You shouldn't go back. Why throw your life away?"

"Saving those you love isn't throwing your life away."

"You barely know us."

"So you have all said time and again." I hold his gaze. "I know you well enough. I won't abandon you, no matter how used you are to that. So get over it."

His brows go up, a flash of shock going through the gray of his eyes. "You really mean it."

"I really mean it." I'm stubborn, and he's only just now starting to realize.

When a slow grin spreads over his lips, it's my turn to realize he doesn't seem to mind.

"Let's go then," he says and takes my hand, curls the fingers of the other one around the watch.

I grab the acorn, feel its by now familiar contours against my palm, the inside of my fingers. "Call for Peter three times, like last time?"

"As many as you want. Not sure that makes any difference.

Not sure the acorn matters, either, or that you need to call out his name at all."

"No?"

"I bet he told you that because he's an arrogant son of a bitch and liked the thought of you screaming his name."

"He wouldn't," I splutter, though it doesn't sound too far-fetched if we're being honest.

Jas winks. Was he being serious or teasing me? "Just close your eyes and think of Neverland."

I can do that.

Clutching the acorn, I close my eyes and think of the island —of their house, now swallowed by the waves, of their faces, of their voices, of their banter and their grins, their boyish laughter and sexy growls, and with them I see Jas, talking with them, fighting for them, bending over me with that snarling shadow—

Air whips around me, wind buffets my face smelling of brine and fish and dead things—and the ground under my feet heaves, sending me stumbling backward.

"Whoa, there." A hand grabs me, steadies me, and I turn to find Jas giving me a grim smile. "There you go."

"It's an earthquake," I gasp, "we need to find shelter—"

"Hardly. You need earth to have an earthquake, if you consider the name of the calamity, at least. But we are on water."

"Water," I repeat dumbly.

But it's true. Seagulls cry, circling overhead, and when I tilt my head back, a little dizzy, I see white clouds sailing across the washed-out sky and... a mast?

"Easy now," he says.

"Where are we?" I whisper, confused. "I thought we were going to the island."

"You mean the lone rock left of it? Barely enough space to sit your ass on there."

"Then where?"

"Welcome on my boat," Jas says, and he's definitely grinning now. He gestures at the sides of the boat, where shadows seem to swirl. "Captain Hook and the Ghostly Crew are at your service."

3

JAS

Wendy is here.

So hard to believe, after all this time mourning my friends, talking only to my ghosts, building the boat from every scrap I found floating around the rock sticking out of the waves.

So hard to credit when I watched her from afar in her world and deemed her happy.

Saved, just like Peter had wanted, like the Lost Boys had wished.

Like I had hoped for.

But I had also hoped to save them, and that failed spectacularly. All these centuries, fighting to spare their lives, and for what?

This pretty girl we barely know.

And yet...

And yet here she is, looking bewildered and confused, barely keeping her feet on my slippery deck, the first living person to set foot on the rickety vessel apart from me, and I'm not even sure I am alive.

I pull her against my chest.

What am I anymore? Who knows? I certainly don't. I hardly know what I feel, and she's soft and warm against me.

"I didn't know you had a boat," she whispers. She sounds out of breath. Shock can do that to you, I know.

"I didn't," I tell her. "I made one. It was that or swim."

She shivers. "*Swim...*"

"I call her Darling."

"Call who?"

I grin. "My boat, of course."

"Oh. Do you, now?" She's wheezing a little.

"In your honor."

"Yeah, so flattered."

"Hey," I protest, "the old girl may be poor but she floats just fine."

"God, I think I'm going to throw up."

Not letting this happen on my deck, so I lead her to the starboard where she clings to the side, bowing over the waves.

"Oh God..." she whispers, retches a little. "This is terrible."

"I know," I say. "We are in the middle of the ocean with only a rock to anchor at, and the next shore belongs to a Fae king who likes to eat small children for breakfast, and what if we get a storm? The boat is small—"

"I meant being at sea," she says. "Though the mermaids lurking right below aren't helping me feel any better."

"Mermaids lurking below?" I frown.

"Can't you see them? Right there—"

I yank her back with a loud curse. "They must have sensed your arrival."

"Oh, goody. Will the good news never stop pouring in? And speaking of which..." She points down, at the water. "What about those cages?"

"What cages?" I pull her away from the side again and make her sit on the bench. "Be careful, Wendy."

"Have you even looked into the sea since the island sank?"

"Of course I have. What are you talking about?" I glance at the waves. "You saw cages? Where?"

"They were right underneath when I was retching."

"Fuck. Show them to me." I sit on the bench beside her, grab he oars. I heave, pull, heave, pull.

Fuck me.

"Didn't you hear them?" she wants to know, and she's reading my thoughts, dammit. "I thought liquid was your medium. That you could spy on anyone through water."

"I could. Past tense. Looks like the Mermaid Queen has taken my ability away. She knows I helped you. Doesn't trust me anymore."

She nods, says nothing. Maybe she's wondering if *she* can trust me.

Not sure I can even trust myself, at this point. I've pretended to be their enemy for so long, there were moments I believed it. When you've played a role for too long, it's hard to remember who you are.

"About... here?" I say, to break the silence, pulling harder on the oars. "Do you see them now?"

Another shiver, but she bends over the side to look. "Not yet."

I row some more, gritting my teeth. "Now?"

"Um... yeah! There they are."

Cages. What the hell.

Abandoning the oars, I join her, careful not to lean over too far and risk capsizing the boat.

A boat. *Ha.* Captain of a *raft* is what I am, roughly fashioned in the shape of a boat, with a small tent to protect us from the rain and the bench we're sitting on.

And now I see them, too. The cages. They are narrow and tall, like pillars, thick chains straining underneath them, probably attaching them to the bottom of the ocean, and inside...

"It's them." She turns huge eyes on me. "It's the Lost Boys."

I'm shaking my head because I don't know if to believe my goddamn eyes, if this is wishful thinking, because they're not dead, they can't be, not if they are imprisoned, and although she had said it, I realize I hadn't believed it, not after mourning them for dead.

"And Peter?" I breathe.

"I don't see him. But it's hard to see through the water."

Especially with the mermaids flashing through, back and forth, barbed fins and serrated tails, scales like chainmail. I grab Wendy and haul her back when one of the merfolk swims too close to the surface.

"I said be careful." I pull her to sit on the bench. "They can jump out of the water and haul you down with them."

"They can climb on the boat, can't they?" She shudders. "Jas...?"

"Don't worry." I grab the oars again. "I'll put spells on the sides."

"Spells. Are you kidding me? You said that you could only travel between worlds."

"Did I?" I shrug. "Maybe I was kidding you. After all, I control an army of shadows."

"True," she breathes, her wide gaze landing on me. "So your watch..."

"Three magical instruments, the acorn, the thimble, and the watch. Sounds like a fairytale, doesn't it?"

"But you said that the acorn wasn't magical."

"No, I said Peter's name wasn't magical. I said magical items help to jump between worlds."

"Oh." She gives a sad little smile. "But my mom's thimble can't have magic. She was... she's..."

"Human?"

"I meant to say *awful*," she says bitterly, looking away. "She's awful. She did things..."

"She was a witch."

"A *bitch*," she corrects me. "She tried to drown me. Threw me off a boat like... like this one. Into the sea. To die. I remember now. recalled it all the right before... right before the island collapsed."

"Fuck, I didn't know. And yeah, that sucks balls." My fucking heart breaks for her. "But I was going to say, I have another source of borrowed magic, so maybe the three magical instruments are bullshit anyway."

"Your shadow," she whispers.

"Yeah. It's not really mine. None of this magic is mine. I used to be a human, too, though it was so long ago I barely remember it." I frown at the rock jutting out of the blue sea, all that's left of the island that was my home for centuries. "Yet, I use it because I figure something has to come out of this goddamn mess, right? I'll make use of what's at my disposal."

"Including me?" She lifts her chin.

"You're the one who insisted to come," I growl, and my shadow rises over me like my own personal dark cloud. "Too late for regrets, princess."

"I don't have any regrets," she shoots back, still in that haughty, defensive voice.

"Not *yet*," I mutter.

But soon she will regret ever seeing me from her window, ever coming back here. Ever wanting to save me. Save us. Has she forgotten how we treated her last time, and the one before?

This is hell, we are her demons, and if she's forgotten, she will remember it any moment now.

THE DAMN CAGES HAUNT MY THOUGHTS. I'D CAUGHT A GLIMPSE of the Twins and Tink, but Wendy is right, I didn't see Peter either.

Which means fucking nothing. Maybe his cage was right out of sight. We didn't linger to look for it.

He has to be there, too. The thought of him being dead is just... impossible, now that the possibility of them being still alive has taken root.

They are alive. Nobody cages corpses, no matter how sick the mermaids might be.

But seeing the faces of the Lost Boys through the water, their hair waving like dead anemones and their eyes closed, I'm not even sure they live.

That was some punch in the gut.

"You said..." I falter, sink down on the bench beside her. "You said you felt them? That they didn't die?"

"That's right."

"They looked dead in those cages," I breathe.

"But they're not. Have some faith, Jas."

"In you?"

"Who else do you have to believe in right now?" she says.

Good point. "I'm not a believer," I warn her. "That was Peter."

"You believed in saving them. All those centuries, you never faltered."

"Until now," I mutter. "Until you told me that they may yet live and... Fuck, I had given up already."

"You couldn't know," she says.

But I should. Of all people, I should be the one to know this. Not her, not a girl we just met, who doesn't really know us.

Then again, Wendy Darling has never been an ordinary girl at all.

"What do we do now?" she asks, glancing uneasily to the side of the boat. "How do we get the Lost Boys out of there?"

"I thought you had a plan," I snap, because I'm annoyed at everything right now. Annoyed I don't have a plan, annoyed I don't have a clue after all this time, annoyed that she's scared and there's nothing I can do to help.

We're rocking gently with the waves, every movement making her greener and paler, and I swear I hear singing, that strange wailing ululation that lifts every hair on my body and makes my teeth grind.

Fucking mermaids.

Not sure whether that's what scares her more or the water. The sea. The memory she recovered, the fear she faced.

The woman that sank the island.

The Wendy we have been waiting for.

"I don't know what to do," she whispers, and her lashes look wet, as if she's trying to keep her tears from spilling. "I have to save them. But how?"

"We have to dive in," I tell her. "See if we can open those cages. Bring them up to the surface."

"I can't." She shakes her head, sniffles a little. The tip of her nose is red and it's strangely endearing. "No way. I can't dive in. I can't swim. Even the thought of going into the water…"

"You can't swim? You serious?"

She shakes her head.

"Damn. I can teach you."

"No! You don't get it, do you? I'm not just *scared* of the sea!" She's breathing hard, her smooth cheeks pale.

"But—"

"I'm frigging terrified!"

"Fuck, okay. It's okay." I lift my hands. "Take a breath."

"I want to go to land," she whispers, her breathing ragged. "Can't stay in this boat. Take me to shore."

"Shore? There's only the rock and—"

"The rock then. Take me there. Now. Please!"

Dammit. She's obviously panicking. What use is it, taking her to the rock in the sea? But maybe she needs to feel steady ground under her feet so she can think rationally again.

Maybe then she'll decide to go back home.

And no matter how much I don't want her to go, it would be

the best for her. Meanwhile, now I know where the others are kept and I'll do my damnedest to get them out myself.

And then... what?

What then, Jas? Brilliant. You get them out of those fucking cages and you all live together happily ever after... on the rock? On your boat? On the shore of a hostile Fae king?

"Jas..." Her voice wobbles. "*Please.*"

I open my mouth to call the ghosts to work but never utter the command. Instead, I take to the oars myself once more and row us to the rock.

For some reason, I can never deny her.

Even if the world ends.

I'm besotted.

What the fuck's wrong with me?

4

WENDY

W e're on a tiny boat.

In the middle of the ocean.

With mermaids swimming underneath.

Is this a joke? All my fears coming together to mock me? Wasn't it enough that I faced and remembered them?

I think I'm going to be sick again. And then maybe pass out for good measure, not to have to deal with the reality of this.

But... the cages. The *boys*.

Remembering how they'd looked, their hair waving in the water, their faces slack, arms dangling at their sides like... like dead limbs.

No.

No, they are not dead. They can't be. I *felt* them. I know I did. I have to get them out of there.

But how?

As we near the high rock jutting out of the sea, I try to sort my panicky thoughts. Dive, Jas had said. Dive into the sea. With some tool, presumably, to break the cage locks.

Jas could do it, though. No need for me. Maybe the whole

purpose of me coming here was to find them, point them out to Jas and watch him bring them out.

Yeah, that's it.

That's what we'll do.

Shivers rack me as the boat lists to one side, then the other. Something bumps against the underside and I swallow a scream.

Jas says nothing, rowing steadily, sculpted muscles working in his arms, sweat shining on his brow, but it's not enough to distract me.

I'm shaking so hard I think I'll rattle my bones loose.

The rock looms in front of us now. Despite what Jas keeps saying, it's pretty big. It's a small island with trees growing on it, a couple leaning precariously over the waves. There are the ruins of buildings, too, a few walls still standing here and there. I think I can make out a house still standing.

Frowning, I hold onto the bench where I'm sitting as Jas brings us closer, wondering why the image makes me cringe.

A beach cabin... waves lapping at the shore... a boat...

Oh. Right.

The rock looms over us, casting shadows on the heaving sea. Seabirds and vultures caw and screech, flying away from their perches to circle over us.

"Here," Jas says, bringing the boat around the island to a sloping beach. Rocks have rolled down to the water's edge, and the way up looks steep. "Sit tight. I'll go out first and pull the boat up—"

But I'm already scrambling out, in a hurry to get out of the boat, out of the water. I jump out, splashing in shallow waves, almost twisting my ankle as I step on uneven rocks—yet it doesn't matter.

All that matters is that I'm on solid ground.

I'm not a total asshole, though, so I turn around and grab

the boat, pulling it with all my strength up the small slope and out of the water.

Jas is cursing under his breath, but he abandons the oars and jumps out, too, helping me. "Would it hurt you physically to do as I say for once?

I grind my teeth and pull. We haul the boat up on the rocky beach and secure it with some rocks.

"I thought," I say as we trudge up the incline to reach the top of the island, "that the entire island was going to sink to the bottom of the sea. But this bit survived."

"There's a memory you haven't retrieved yet," he says. "A fear you haven't faced. That's why."

The idea that I'm inextricably bound to this heap of rocks, that my fears and dreams are its bones and flesh, still shocks the hell out of me—and yet I believe it. Nothing makes sense, and yet this makes the most sense anything ever has.

This island is my mind. It's me.

We pass two scraggly trees. There are bones littered underneath them that I don't want to examine more closely. Human bones? Animal bones? Whatever they are, the vultures must have picked them clean.

"What happened to the Reds?" I ask. "Are they all gone?"

"Haven't seen anything move on the surface since the rest of the island went down." Jas gives me a hand crossing a deep crack in the ground. "They'd be hard to miss."

True. Red mechanical giants, operating on magic, wearing alternatingly the face of my mother and then my father.

That had been so frigging creepy.

And now... "What's that?" I point past the rocks and struggling trees at something red and eye-catching.

Which turns out to be the carcass of a car.

Jas frowns. "I don't remember ever seeing that car here before. Does it mean anything to you?"

"Well... We used to have a car like this, back then," I

whisper. "I hated it. I used to imagine that the engine would fail and we'd die in a horrific accident."

"I guess now we know where the metal parts of the Reds came from," he says, "and to what they have returned now you have faced the memory."

I want to laugh and scorn his words, the very idea, but... What if he's right? Did I create the Reds mixing my memories of that car and my parents with a dash of nightmare?

I can believe it. Everything else is crazy enough already.

"Wendy..." Jas grabs my arm, stops me in my tracks. His gray eyes are shadowed. "What are we doing here on the rock? I know you're afraid of the sea, but we're in the middle of the ocean. It's swim or drown. You can't help anyone like this. Maybe it's time you went back home."

"No." I shake my head for emphasis. "No, I have to help them."

"How?" He regards me gravely. "*Remembering* your fears isn't enough. Facing them requires more than awareness of them."

"What do you mean?" I glance again, helplessly, at the remains of the car.

"I mean, you need to get back in the saddle."

I swallow hard. "Jas..."

"Get your feet wet. Take the plunge. Swim against the tide."

"Very funny, Jas," I choke out.

"I wasn't trying to be funny."

"Well, good, because you're not." I pull my hand free, and to be fair he lets me go. I stomp uphill until I'm at the summit of the rock and turn in a slow circle.

Water.

Only water all around us as far as the eye can see—though I think I make out distant mountains in one direction.

"What is that shore?" I point.

"One of the Fae kingdoms," Jas says, coming to stand next to me. "The Night Mountains. Tink's father is king there."

"Fae," I whisper. "Do they look like us? Are their ears pointed like Tink's get when he gets annoyed??"

"I would say their ears are the least disturbing thing about them," Jas says darkly.

I squint at the jagged line at the horizon. "And they never sent a ship to see what happened here? Didn't the king want to know what happened to his son?"

"He never cared to meet Tink. Why would he start caring now?"

"Crap. Poor Tink. His father sucks." I gesture at the ground under our feet. "What about the island? Isn't it important?"

"It was," Jas says, "while it existed. Now the bridge has collapsed and the Fae have laid their fear of it to rest."

"But it's not all gone!"

"No, it isn't. They probably think it is, though." His turn to swallow, the knot in his throat bobbing. "Through my shadow, they sensed my loss, my grief. They think it's all over."

His handsome face is grim, the shadows in his normally light eyes darker. Losing Peter and the Boys seems to have shattered him.

"That's why you went to them," I whisper. "To the dark Fae. You sought out their alliance to protect the Lost Boys from the nightmares and monsters while trying to find a way to keep them alive. Your fear was losing them. Did you...? It's so hard to ask this, so hard to know. "Did you kill the other Wendies? To stop them from sinking the island?"

A chuckle escapes him. "You really think I'd do something like that?"

"Your shadow isn't exactly human."

He sobers quickly. "I never killed any of the girls. They went mad and jumped to their deaths. It was a sad affair. And speaking of fears... Isn't it high time you battled your own?" he prods. "That you learned to move in the water so you can never be in danger of drowning again?"

"Except for the mermaids, of course." I bare my teeth at him. "And the sharks and other hungry things." And now I feel bad for accusing him of murder. "Listen, Jas—"

"The mermaids don't want to eat you. The one they want is Peter and they got him."

"Okay, but—"

"Stay here, then. I'll go free them. But if I don't make it back…"

"Don't say that," I whisper, "you will come back, you—"

"We don't know that," he counters. Taking the watch out of his waistcoat pocket, he hands it to me. "Take it. If I don't come back… use it. Use it to escape, to go back home."

"No." I'm shaking my head even as he pushes the watch into my hands. "I don't want it. I don't want to go."

He sighs. "Fuck, I don't want you to go, either. Stupid, huh? I want you safe but at the same time I want you here, with me."

"No, it's not stupid," I whisper, touched by his admission. "But, Jas…" On impulse, I throw my arms around him. "You have to come back."

And he kisses me.

He kisses me like he's the one drowning and I'm sweet balmy air, like he's dying and I'm life. I moan, clinging to him, everything he did to me, all the pleasure he shoved into me returning in my memory in excruciating minute detail.

And I remember how it was with the other boys, too, and I…

I break away. "Okay," I whisper.

"Okay, what?"

"Teach me how to swim. It's time."

Time to brave the waves.

5

WENDY

Loose pebbles slide under our feet as we make our way back down—on the other side of the island this time.

All that dark, angry blue heaving around us makes my stomach clench. It's like a monster, that primordial snake surrounding the world, threatening to swallow it whole.

"What made you change your mind?" Jas asks, grabbing me before I freefall all the way down into the water, and God, that would have been my end, because my heart would stop right then and there.

"I've gone crazy," I say, my voice all wheezy. "Don't you think it was about time?"

"Join our exclusive club," he laughs. "I'll prepare your membership card now."

I try to smile but fear has my stomach in a giant knot as we step on the rocks scattered like candies at the edge of the water. He leads me from the one to the next, his tread sure and steady, his grip on my hand hard and strong.

We stop at a small rock pool into which water whooshes and then slides back out.

"Here we are," he says. "This is a good spot."

"I didn't bring my swimsuit," I hedge, my nerves getting the better of me.

"Skinny dipping is all the rage."

"You just want to see me naked."

"Yes," he says, honesty shining in his voice. No lies, no pretexts, no hiding in any way. His eyes crinkle at the corners. "I'm dying to see you naked. Though…" He shrugs his powerful shoulders. "That's not the way I had imagined fucking you again."

My mouth goes dry and my heart starts to race. "What did you imagine?"

Anything to avoid thinking about the water lapping at the rocks, sending ripples through the small pool.

"I'd lay you down," he says, "kiss you, tear your clothes off you and…" His shadow flares like a black mantle, whipping up as if blown by a strong wind, rising over his head. His voice deepens, drops to a growl. "And then I'd spread you and use my belt to lash at your pussy, until you scream, until you cry and shake, until you come just from that."

Warmth seeps into my face, and okay, now I'm starting to get very distracted. "Jas…"

"Undress, now," he commands me, his eyes turning a solid black, his teeth looking sharp, turning his charming grin into a predator's bite. "Or I'll shred everything off you."

With trembling hands, I hurry to obey, unzipping my jeans and shoving them down, kicking off my shoes and socks. I grab the hem of my sweater and pull it over my head, let it drop to the ground.

"Yeah, that's right." His tongue darts out, swiping over his lips, and he advances on me. "Take it all off. Everything."

God. I'm so aware of his hot, dark gaze on me, I barely remember the heaving sea behind me. I feel like I'm burning, despite the cold breeze coming off the ocean.

He unclasps my bra and pulls it off, yanks down my panties, leaving me bared.

When he sweeps me off my feet and swings me up in his arms, I swallow a cry.

And then he steps into the water, still dressed, and we sink until I'm clutching at him, all wet and frozen to the bone in the rock pool. My nipples ache, hard as pebbles. My skin frigging hurts.

"Damn," he says, and when I glance up, I find his eyes have gone back to that pale gray. "It's fucking cold."

"Was all that a distraction?" I whisper, snickering. "To get me into the water?"

"What was? No." His jaw clamps tight. "Not a distraction."

It doesn't matter. It worked. I'm in the water, in his arms, and I'm not freaking out.

Well, not yet.

And his pale eyes start to darken again as he looks down at me, buck naked against him, pressed to his chest, and I feel the bulge of his hard cock against my side. It's so hot, it seems to burn through the wet fabric of his pants, searing my chilled flesh.

"You're the one who's distracting," he says, that low, grating growl still in his voice.

"You're the one who told me to undress."

"Advice I should have followed, too." His mouth twists in a rueful smile, and he sinks lower in the water, grunting when I tighten my hold on him. "Relax, sweets. I've got you."

"You don't... understand..." My teeth are chattering, half from cold, half from fear. "I can't..."

"Yes, you can. You're here. The sea wants you to float. Salty water pushes you up, see? If you relax a little, you'll float."

"Not true," I wheeze. "I almost drowned once. I sank. It was dark. Hands were pulling on me—"

"You can drown in two feet of water if you panic." He

unwraps one of his arms from around me and I hang on to him with all my might. He grips my chin, lifts it just enough to meet my eyes. "What must have seemed to you like fucking hours as you sank were probably seconds until Peter got to you. All right?"

"Nothing's *all right*! Jas…"

"Let go of me, girl. I promise I got you. Trust me, okay? I'm the only person you can trust in this world right now. *Let go*."

"I can't. No way." I can't breathe. "This is too much."

But I must.

For the Lost Boys.

For myself.

So I let go.

And flounder.

Gasp.

Start sinking.

His hand under my back pushes me back up and I splutter, coughing salty water. "Now move your arms and legs. Motion also keeps you floating. Try it."

I want to cry out I can't, and it's already a lot and what use will it be?—but I do as he says, frantically waving my arms and legs in the water.

His hand is still there—then it isn't—but before I can panic all over again, it returns, supporting me, guiding me. His other hand comes against my belly and slowly moves me forward until I'm prone, fighting the water, trying not to swallow any.

"Calm down," he says. "Let the fucking ocean simply be, and calm your thoughts. Nothing can touch you here. I'm holding you. Feel it?"

I feel it, but this won't be a switch to flip and make everything okay. I'm getting tired—mostly from the emotion clogging my throat, filling up my chest.

"Enough. And now," he says, grinning that sharp, sexy grin, "let's get back to the distraction…"

———

I'VE NEVER HAD SEX IN THE WATER. NEVER WAS ON MY BUCKET list, not even in a hot tub or the shower, let alone in the dreaded ocean.

Yet here I am, because he's peeling his drenched shirt off his ripped chest and I can't think about anything other than the hard planes of his abs and pecs, the droplets lovingly tracing every ridge and line on their way down.

A scar runs down his side, similar to Peter's but not quite the same, not angry and red but white and old—and I'm distracted again by his perfection. It's unreal how boldly sculpted his chest is, and I've turned out to be sucker for muscular guys. They turn me on in a way no man I've been with ever has.

Muscular, handsome, mysterious and violent psychos in a world that shouldn't exist and yet here I am, ogling Jas as he strips for me in the shallows of the pool. I ache between my legs and all I can think of is him taking me, the thought overriding the panic attack I nearly had in the water.

What gives, right?

It doesn't matter, not when he starts work on his pants, unbuttoning them and shoving them down his lean hips, proving he's wearing no briefs or anything, down his thick thighs and *oh dear loving God...*

I never got a chance to see his body or his cock last time, when he fucked me.

I see everything now, and the sea, what sea? Who cares? If this is the cure to my panic attacks, then yes please, I'll take the pill. Hell, I'll take the whole pill bottle.

He's like a drug.

A six-foot-and-five ripped, handsome drug I'll take willingly, let it blot out my memories and fears.

When he grabs me and hauls me against him, I wrap my

legs around him. His hand lifts to my throat, closes over my windpipe, then his mouth covers mine, stealing the rest of my air.

Meanwhile, his other hand grips my ass, squeezing, then his fingers dip between my legs and plunge into my pussy.

Rough. Demanding. Thrusting in and out, not leaving me a chance to move or make a sound.

I squirm, fight to break the kiss, but he bites on my lip, startling me, just as his fingers thrust deeper—and I come, shaking, not even feeling the water, not feeling anything but the all-consuming rush of pleasure.

Oh my God, so good...

With a last bite on my lips, he draws back, eyes burning in his handsome face. He relaxes his hold on my neck, letting me breathe.

Then he yanks his fingers out before I'm done coming, reaches between us and guides his cock into me.

I'm still clenching inside as his huge cock rams into me and I yell, half in pleasure and half in discomfort as he fills me up, an inexorable drive, deeper and deeper until he's in all the way.

His face is twisted in anger or pain or ecstasy as he gazes down at me, impossible to tell with the shadow writhing around him, obscuring his features, but his teeth flash—a grin, a grimace.

He shoves me against the rocks and bows over me, hips snapping, his grip on my hips painful, more growling escaping him as he fucks me hard, taking his own pleasure, his terrible shadow snarling over him, reaching for me, slicing through me...

Throwing my head back, this time I scream as I come, the fear and the panic meshing with the burn and pleasure of my second release, plunging me into blackness.

6

PETER

She's here.

Here in this world.

Wendy Darling.

I can feel it in my gut, in my bones. Twisting about in my heavy chains, inside the Mermaid Queen's palace, I keep glancing around as if I'll see her walking toward me.

No chance of that. Even if I was outside the walls of the palace and not under its vaulted coral ceilings, she wouldn't be there.

Wendy is terrified of water, of the sea.

So why do I sense her near?

And why is she back? Surely it isn't for a bunch of losers like us? Or for a junkie, like me?

I should be furious with her. Hell, I *am* furious. I did my best to save her, to give her another chance at life, and she comes back where she will most probably die alongside us.

But I can't help the happiness I feel at the thought of seeing her again.

Dammit.

Something's broken in me. Something that kept me going,

that kept my dark heart safe all these endless years, and she's the one who did it. She fucking broke me.

And now she's back.

"Peter," the Queen says. "You're not paying attention."

Ignoring the frissons racing through my body, I turn back to her. Her terrible countenance isn't any fucking better from up close, let me tell you. She's sort of curled up in a massive chair, a throne of sorts, her pearly tail twisting below her, blue eyes burning like fires in her skull-like face.

"You haven't yet told me why the hell I'm here."

"Instead of lying dead at the bottom of the sea, fodder for the fish?" she asks sweetly.

But I'm not Wendy. I'm not afraid of the sea and its creatures—or of death. "Damn right."

"Would you have preferred that?"

I open my mouth to curse her and her ancestors, but then I remember my friends in the cages outside the palace and grit my teeth instead. It's not only my life at stake. "Just curious," I finally mutter.

"Pretending you didn't know I wanted you here all this time?"

"Here at the palace?" I hedge.

"Here by my side."

"I'm not a merman or a Fae," I say as evenly as I can manage. "Not sure what use you think you might have for me."

"Nobody has a shadow like you, Peter. Nobody has power like you."

"Power?" I laugh bitterly and lift my manacled hands, making the chains clank. "What power?"

"I wouldn't want it if it was out of hand, now, would I?"

"What are you talking about?"

"You know what I'm talking about. All of you have magic. But you are their center, now that the annoying girl has been sent back and that business of mending or breaking the island is over and done with, at long last. Without her, you are stronger. Without her, you can be the man you were meant to be."

I can't help it, I laugh again. "Go, villain monologues. Is this supposed to turn me to your side?"

"What if your shadow could be mended?" she says, probably not even noticing the irony of it all. She'd be hilarious if she wasn't a monster.

God, I'd fucking kill for a smoke right now.

"My shadow is human," I tell her. "Mortal. Not sure what use it would be to you, mended or not."

"It's not mortal anymore. You are not a mortal anymore, and you know it. You never were, Peter Pan. Otherwise... how would you still be alive?"

"Are you saying... that us being alive is not your doing?"

Her eyes narrow. "Is it possible that you don't know who you really are? No... that's ridiculous."

"Spare me your riddles. I'm Peter Pan, that's who I am."

"Peter Pan..." The sound she produces is reminiscent of a laugh. "Don't tell me that you forgot?"

"Well, my recollection ain't what it once was," I drawl. "Funny what a couple shitty centuries can do to you. Refresh my memory, why don't you?"

Even if I'm not entirely sure I want to know.

The gleam in her eyes is fucking unnerving.

"Oh no, it wouldn't do for me to tell you such things," she says. "Spoil the fun. No wonder you've been so easy to capture and hold. No wonder you let the island collapse and failed in your mission. Besides, I quite like you like this. So obedient and helpless."

"I didn't fail my mission," I mutter, "I broke the fucking bridge between the worlds, broke the nightmare—"

"That didn't work out so well, though, did it? With a piece of the island still standing?" Her voice has gone soft, probing. Gloating. "You did fail."

No, not possible. "A piece still standing? What do you mean?"

She ignores my questions. "And that wasn't all, was it? Not the whole mission. Waiting all these centuries just for a girl, a specific girl..."

What does she mean, it wasn't the end mission? Of course it was. Sinking the island, sending Wendy back... What else was there?

And fuck, why can't I remember?

She's talking about Wendy—but her return isn't my fault. I did all I could to send her back. Is her return my failure, too?

I glare at the Queen from under my wet bangs. They move a little in the currents going through the palace.

My first reaction is to think she's goading me, lying to me just to get under my skin—but I have a niggling doubt at the back of my mind that she's right.

That I had another mission, a mission I forgot, and it has to do with Wendy, and yet...

Fuck...

"Since I failed," I grind out, "how about you let the others go? Looks like I'm the one you want."

She laughs. It's an evil cackle, or maybe that's the distortion in the water, but the sound grates inside my head like the screeching of nails on a board. "You didn't really believe that line would work."

"What the fuck do you want from me?" I turn away from her, gazing once more at my friends, frustration and worry eating at me.

Suspended in the cages, upright but not quite conscious—maybe not quite alive, for all I know, and the sight is another punch to the guts.

"A child," she says.

A snort escapes me in a burst of bubbles that tickle my lips. "You're fucking kidding me. You want a child?"

"It has been prophesied that Peter Pan's offspring will control the gates between the worlds."

"And you want that child for yourself." I turn back toward her and swallow a gasp when I find her right in front of me.

She's floating in the water as if in midair, her hair like green seaweed moving around her face, her sharp teeth bared as if she's about to take a chunk out of me.

"I won't ask for the child, Peter Pan," she says. "You will give it to me."

"Why would I?"

"I can be very persuasive." A small fish escapes from the corner of her mouth and swims away. "A child or your friends die."

So they are still alive. Hope fills me.

"See now why I won't even have to ask twice. I will bear that baby, raise it to be loyal to me, do my bidding. Much more practical than kidnapping a child."

"You..." The *fuck*. She's about to use me as a sperm donor and I doubt she'll even ask me if I'm in the mood. Which would be never, by the way. I want to laugh, barely holding back. "This is fucking ridiculous. You fucking can't."

"Watch me," she says, another fish escaping her mouth.

It sends a goddamn shiver of revulsion through me. "You'd use your own child. You truly are a fucking monster."

"Oh, come off it. There are higher stakes to consider here. Besides, I never pegged you as a romantic. Going all sentimental over the possibility of a child, after sending the Darling girl back to her world, letting her destroy the island to save her life. A romantic fool. Was that part of your grand scheme?"

I clench my jaw. Memory is a fragmented, tortured thing

but I'm sure sending Wendy away *was* my plan, though this outcome wasn't what I'd expected.

I'd expected to die, me and the others, not be caged, fucking *used* against our will.

What the fuck, seriously. What's going on here? I wish my head wasn't so fuzzy, so fucked up.

Why did I ever think that sending Wendy back and sinking the island, saving the worlds, might rid me of this curse?

Why did I think that Wendy would stay away, safe and sound, and that we, at least, would have a clean death, when my friends are in cages instead and I'm about to be raped by the Mermaid Queen?

And above everything, what the hell did I miss in my plans and *why*? What was I thinking?

Someone out there must be laughing his head off. Whoever that is, they owe me answers and I intend to get them.

7

WENDY

We have set up temporary camp on the lone rock of the island, lit a fire, and Jas' ghostly soldiers brought us some fish they caught. Jas scaled and gutted them, then spitted them on twigs he cleaned with a knife and made a fire over which he placed them to cook.

A proper boy scout.

He's folded his tall body, knees drawn in, broad shoulders hunched. He's quiet, staring into the flames, all pale eyes and hair and skin, all sharp lines and angles, his shadow barely there.

"How do you think they breathe?" I whisper as the fish crackle over the low flames, dripping juices. "Underwater?"

"Magic," he says drily, his mouth twisting. "What else?"

"Their own magic or the mermaids'?"

"Just how magical do you think we are?"

"Tink has magic." I shrug. His watch seems to weigh a ton, attached to a belt loop at the waist of my jeans, dragging me down. "I had understood that all of you do, magical items or not."

His eyes have gone distant. He pokes at the burning wood

with a stick. "Yeah, we have magic, don't we? But it seems to be locked somewhere deep inside of us, like the fire inside a dormant volcano. However, them kept in cages, breathing underwater, sounds rather like a case of merfolk sorcery."

"Well, it is a good thing if it keeps them alive," I whisper. "You make it sound like a curse."

He stabs the stick into the embers. The flames jump in his eyes. "Mermaids don't pull their power from the elements, from the energies passing through the world, moving it. They draw it from living things, draining them, killing them."

"So... to keep Peter and the Boys alive, they are killing someone else, is that what you're saying? Who?"

"Haven't got the faintest idea." He looks tired, faint smudges under his eyes, his mouth drawn tight. "All this time we avoided the mermaids like the plague they are, instead fighting with each other and against the Reds. We kept out of the water as much as possible. Even the shadows were afraid to get close."

"And yet you can swim," I whisper. "And build boats, and navigate under the stars."

"Old knowledge," he says. "Old habits."

I look at his young, unlined face, so handsome in the flickering light of the fire, and I almost laugh, but stop myself in time. Old? What is he saying?

Sometimes I forget how long these guys have been here, at least according to their own accounts. How long Jas has been fighting and hoping and despairing.

"You never told me why you and Peter stabbed each other," I say.

He glances up at that. "What?"

"If you like him and the Boys so much, if all you have said is true and you have been fighting them all this time to save them from themselves, from sinking the island and dying—then how come you stabbed him?"

"We had a fight," he says after a long moment. "About one

of the first Wendies he brought over. She wasn't the one, that much was fucking obvious, but Peter wanted it to work, he was so hopeful... I thought... I thought there wasn't a right one, but he wouldn't listen. God above. That happened... a fucking lifetime ago."

"And you both have the scars to prove it," I whisper. "Peter's... he seems to hurt when his shadow distorts, pulling like a stitch coming loose from the edge of a deep wound, and yours..."

"You know nothing about mine," he grits out.

"Does yours hurt, too?"

"When he stabbed me... it killed my human shadow. The Lost Boys think I exchanged my shadow for a Fae leech on purpose, they think I chose to be here, in this goddamn mess. But that fight with Peter changed me forever, it opened a wound in me that never healed, where this fucking alien shadow attached itself afterward, and I... Fuck. Fuck!"

"What's the matter?"

"The *matter*?" he breathes. "*Everything* is the fucking *matter*." He throws the stick into the flames and gets up. "Sitting here on our asses, reminiscing bad times and speculating about the nature of magic isn't helping. Cooking fish and playing house. As if we're a couple of kids. I should get going before night falls."

I swallow hard. "Wait, Jas..."

"I need to get to them, haul them out of those cages." He takes a few steps back, shaking his head. "Being with you is always distracting, it takes my mind off the bad things, off the things that have to get done, no matter the cost. It's dangerous, being around you. You're dangerous."

So is he, so are all of them—to my mind, to my heart, and I realize as I stand there, reaching for him, that I can't do it.

I can't stay put, eat flaky fish and lie under the deep sky, knowing Jas will be out there, diving into the ocean, trying to free the others, trying to save them.

So I get up.

He frowns at me. "Where are you going?"

"I'm coming with you."

———

"I THOUGHT YOU WERE TERRIFIED OF BOATS AND THE WATER," HE says, his gaze narrowed.

"I am. And yet I had a swimming lesson with you."

"Among other things," he mutters, one side of his mouth twitching as he pushes the boat into the water and helps me climb in it.

"True."

Okay, so he took my mind off my fear earlier, but now it's getting even worse because we're sailing right over the mermaid city, or prison, or whatever it is.

Right over it, in this tiny boat, and Jas will jump into the sea, leaving me alone to wait and wonder if I'll ever see him alive again.

If I'll see any of them again.

I will wonder if the mermaids won't jump into the vessel, magic wards or not, grab me and eat me.

Or worse still, drag me down into the murky depths that haunt my nightmares.

The boat rocks and I barely swallow a squeal, holding on to the side for dear life. "Watch what you're doing, Jas!"

He frowns as he pulls on the oars. "We're fine, sweetheart."

"Are we?" The boat rocks again and Jas pauses in his rowing.

"It's mermaids," he says.

Shit.

"We need to move faster," he decides and bends back to the oars. "Men, stand watch at the sides!"

This time I squeal out loud when the shadows gather around us, becoming dense, taking the shape of men, long black swords appearing in their hands, their eyes flashing with cold fire.

Ghosts.

They died but now they are trapped in this twilight world. Much like Jas. Much like Peter and the Lost Boys.

I broke the bridge but they are still trapped. Is it because a part of the island is still standing?

You have one last fear to face...

The shadow men slash the air with their opaque swords, and a scream echoes. It's an inhuman sound, raising every small hair on my body.

I bow over my legs, hugging my knees.

This was your choice, coming back to Neverland, getting into this boat, I tell myself. *Get over your fear. Let it go. It's time.*

I should be on shore, on the island. Why the hell did I join Jas for this? He doesn't need me.

And yet you feel that you should be here, that you are needed, that you can't sit this rescue out. Can't be a coward, can't keep hiding and expect others to save you.

Jas just keeps rowing, his handsome face set in stone, powerful muscles flexing in his arms, silver hair falling in his eyes.

"Peter wasn't in a cage," I whisper. My teeth are chattering, and I keep talking to distract myself. "Why wasn't he in a cage? Because he is the king? Because the Mermaid Queen wanted him? Or because he's dead—deader than the others? Maybe he doesn't do water, maybe salt doesn't sit well with him, maybe—"

"*Wendy,*" Jas says, his voice sharp.

"Sorry, sorry. Keep rowing, I'm okay, just thinking out loud."

Another hit against the side of the boat makes me hiss. "It could be important that Peter isn't in a cage, unless we just didn't happen to see his cage, but let's say he's not in the same situation as the others, like—"

"The difference could be important," Jas says, his piercing gaze locking with mine. "Is that what you're saying?"

"You have three boys in cages and one outside, one that the Queen wants as a consort, one that is more powerful than the others, and—"

"What if they're draining the Lost Boys to keep Peter alive? They keep them breathing but little by little they suck them dry?"

"Like batteries," I agree. "Yeah, that's what I was thinking."

"Fuck," he breathes, laying down the oars, brows drawn together.

"Fuck, exactly, I agree. What about the Queen? What will it mean, making Peter her consort?"

"I don't fucking know," he says, "but it can't be anything good."

"Exactly my thoughts, though I had hoped you might have a better idea, being so old and all."

His mouth twitches. "Are you seriously making fun of me right now?"

"Not really." I give him a tiny smile. "I'm just out of sorts."

He scrubs his hands over his face. They are covered in old scars. "She wants his power, but Peter... Peter may not even remember his power, may not even have his original might anymore. It's complicated."

"Weren't you going to tell me what he is? What all of you really are?"

His brows wing up. "You mean apart from tortured, damaged guys who are into rough sex, guns and knives?"

"Yeah, that."

He opens his mouth, either to reply or to retort, most probably, when the boat rocks violently.

I scream, grabbing at the bench, and Jas's gray eyes widen more as he tips over the side.

He just tips into the sea, falling bodily, without a splash, hands grabbing at him, at his hair, his shoulders, his arms—white, skeletal hands I only see for a brief moment—

And he's gone, followed by eerie quiet.

What just happened?

"No. No! Please." I clutch the side of the boat, looking down, my breath shuddering out of me. "Jas!" I scream. "Jas, no! Don't leave me alone!"

But he's gone under the waves.

They've caught him, too.

What do I do now? This wasn't the plan, wasn't how it was supposed to go.

And so what? Are you going to sit here and cry?

No.

Can't let them have him.

Can't let them have any of my boys.

You're not going to jump into the sea, though, are you? That'd be crazy.

I still don't know how to swim.

I'm still terrified.

But if I'm here, I'm here for a reason, and thinking rationally about any of this isn't helping. Hasn't helped so far. Only made me fear more.

So I refuse to think about it anymore. I swing my legs off the side of the boat, and jump in.

Into the cold. Into the dark.

Taking the plunge, as Jas had said.

I sink in dark water.

8

WENDY

I'm sinking, the black water sucking me down, drowning me, killing me. I'm falling down the rabbit hole, a black hole that has no bottom.

Fish swim past as I swirl gently, my eyes wide open, arms spread wide. Shadows slither around me, whispering, asking, murmuring.

I expect clawed hands to reach for me, grab my ankles, pull me down.

I expect to see fanged mouths opening, snapping at me.

I expect pain, and suffocation, and death, but so far, I'm only drifting downward. It's as if I'm not moving through water but thick air.

As if this is a dream.

That thought slices right through the fog in my mind and I jerk like a fish on a hook. Is this a dream? Am I in my bed, asleep, imagining this place? How can I wake myself up from his nightmare?

I pinch my skin, about to test the theory but then I think... Would that be good or bad?

In theory, if I'm asleep, if I dreamed all this up... then I never met the boys. Or they are dead, drowned and dead. And if this is real... then I did meet them, and I do feel the things I feel for them, and I will do all I can to save them.

But what if I met them in a dream? What if waking up erases them? My feelings exist and won't go away.

I release my skin without pressing it between my fingers. I don't want to know, not now. I should be hoping that I'm dreaming, wishing for it, praying to wake up. But instead, I hope that this is all real. That I'm breathing underwater, that I am somehow meant to be here.

Or that it's a dream I never wake up from, a dream where I find them and save them and stay with them.

Dream or not, my pants are stuck to my legs, and my sweater feels so heavy, probably what's dragging me down. That day with my parents... I'd worn a long sweater then, too, and boots, and jeans, like now and...

Focus, Dee.

You're not a child anymore.

That was another time. You have chosen this.

And if you chose it, if can breathe and move, then you can control this descent into hell.

You have to.

All right.

My dream, right? That was what Peter told me. My nightmare. Because this place is me, it's the inside of my head, distorted and twisted but no more than it already was, just... different.

More tangible.

Easier to grapple with.

Turning my head, I see the shadows again, but they don't drift any closer as I swirl downward. Bright lights swirl with me, like stars, and I pass my hands through them, dissipating them, breaking them up into glitter.

It reminds me of Charlie and the party where I met her. She had been half covered in glitter and had left shiny kisses on the faces of most boys in the room.

Then she discovered me and made it her mission to draw me out of my shell. She decided I needed to have fun. Doctor's prescription, she'd said, and she'd made it her life's mission to see me happy after that.

The memory makes me smile.

And I choke on water.

The memory of almost drowning closes in on me, the panic and fear of the end. I'm not ready, not ready to die...

And then I see the hands reaching for me—Peter's hands, his pale face in the water, eyes dark and wide as he drags me up, to the surface.

I draw a shaky breath.

See, Dee? Not drowning.

Not sinking into memories, into the past. I made it out. I made it here.

The shadows flit away. The water clears, azure, teal, cobalt, crystal glass with silver streaks of lightning.

I see below me the cages and then...

The palace.

———

IT DOESN'T LOOK LIKE A PALACE BUT I KNOW THIS IS THE Mermaid Queen's abode.

I can feel it.

And I mean, what else can it be? It's obviously a structure, all organic curves and pale colors, twisting in and out of itself like the tentacles of an octopus, changing colors like a hunting squid, labyrinthine passages burrowing into sinister mounts with spikes that glint like glass and metal. It's huge, its size becoming more apparent as I sink lower and lower. It spreads in every direction, in width and height and depth.

But my attention is on the cages.

A forest of cages, tall, narrow constructions resembling hollow pillars made of intricate black lace, the beehive tops supported on thick bars running from top to bottom.

Just how many people are the mermaids keeping imprisoned under the sea, possibly using them to extract energy for their magic?

Or perhaps to eat them whenever they feel peckish, who really knows?

Like energy snacks. Something to keep you going through the day.

Focus, Dee, focus. You're not being very funny right now.

Right. I know.

Well, if I can breathe underwater, then fine. Time to stop questioning how this is possible, how all this is real. Because it is.

And it's time to free my boys.

I turn toward the forest of cages and kick my arms and legs the way Jas showed me in the rocky pool. I don't expect it to actually work but it does, the movements propelling me forward through the water.

I flail a little. It's my first time moving purposefully through water—through life, to be honest—and it takes a little getting used to. Getting used to moving in an element that has terrified me for such a long time I can't really remember the time before.

The cages glint faintly in the cobalt sea, a shiny copper and silver. They are like tree trunks, denuded of their branches and foliage, and silver fish shoals roam over them like swarms of insects or flocks of small birds.

I shouldn't be able to observe everything with such detachment. It's as if time has slowed down, reality has fractured into still images and I'm moving through it a frame at a time.

Then I'm passing over the nearest cages and I dive lower so I can swim between them, looking into each one, looking for my Lost Boys.

When I approach the first cage, reaching for the gilded bars, I flinch.

"Christ!" Bubbles escape my mouth when I gasp, my stomach turning over, because the woman trapped inside looks more like a corpse than a person. Her bones show through her pale skin, her clothes hang off her in tatters, and her long locks weave in the water like dead tentacles. Her eyes are open and filmed over.

No, no... Frantic, I swim between more cages, glancing right and left.

It's like a cemetery, the people inside looking very dead, unless they are zombies about to wake up and grab me through the bars, take a bite out of me.

This second thought is even less reassuring than the first.

I knew I shouldn't have watched all those zombie series with Charlie.

And the thought brings back the fear. What if I'm too late? What if my Boys are already dead?

My pulse thumping behind my collarbone, closing my throat, I move faster, as fast as I dare while checking every cage, flinching at every movement I catch out of the corner of my eye, fully expecting the dead to come back to life.

As I move away from the palace, among the cages, I find people who start looking more alive. More recent acquisitions? Many of them have very delicate features and their ears look... weird. Weirdly pointed. Wait a minute...

Are they Fae?

Apparently, there are Fae in this world—which I knew, just didn't want to fully accept.

In fact, this world is Faerie and the island was a bridge between the worlds that Peter was all too happy to see gone.

Fae and human prisoners, rotting away in cages at the bottom of a strange sea.

I need to get out of here, I need to find the Boys and escape with them—but...

Peter.

Jas.

And all those prisoners who may still be alive.

I'm breathing hard, my heart banging against my ribs, as I pull myself from bar to bar and from cage to cage, steeling myself to face more and more emaciated faces and bodies, eyes that never turn to find me.

How the hell are the mermaids doing it? In fact, are they doing anything, are they really sucking the life out of these people or are they simply leaving them here to die? Is it a form of sick torture?

Why go into the trouble of making these beautiful cages, though? Surely there are cheaper forms of torture.

As if I understand torture.

As if I understand this world and its creatures.

But you do, a voice says inside my head and it sounds suspiciously like Tink's. *You put your stamp on this world. It was made from your dreams. The creatures here have behaviors you understand because they came from your subconscious.*

God. Tink. Colt and Wes. Peter and Jas. Where are they all?

Just when I start to lose my energy and momentum, when I start to lose faith that I'll ever see them again, I grab the bars of a shiny cage and jolt to a halt. The sea currents buffet me much like the wind had always done on the island, threatening to tear me away, but I hold on for dear life.

Wesson.

His face is pale and beautiful in the dark water, as if carved from marble, eyes and mouth closed, his golden hair floating about his head like the halo of some young saint. His arms are loose by his sides, his knees slightly bent.

"Wes. Wes!" I reach between the bars to touch him. "Can you hear me? Wake up, Wes! Where are the others? I came to set you free!"

9

WES

A voice. I'm hearing a sweet voice I thought I'd never hear again. It's out of place here and yet it's exactly the one I'd been wishing and hoping for.

But I'm lost in a maze of streets and paths that turn into corridors and rooms, and I wander, searching, yelling for Colt and for anyone to open the door and let me out.

I'm in one of the foster homes I spent time in.

Dark days. Sleepless nights. Pain and suppressed tears, suppressed screams.

The bullies roll over me, one by one, from the foster parents to the social workers to the kids staying in the house with me. Broken bones, broken hopes. Drugs and hazy moments, trying to drown out the aches and fears.

The loneliness.

The fucking hopelessness.

Goddammit. I'd promised myself never to go back there, so why? Why the fuck am I wandering this house again?

Colt. I need to find Colt, find someone to tell me where he was taken, why he vanished, why he never wrote or called. If he's still alive.

So I start moving, make myself move. The lamps overhead flicker and buzz. Insects die and fall, inert, to the floor that's covered in them. A thin carpet that cushions my steps. The air is thick like molasses, like water.

There's a pressure on my chest with every breath I draw. But that's normal. That pressure has been there for as long as I can remember. Since Colt and I got split up. Since—

"Wes!" the voice calls out once more and I stop in my tracks.

Slowly turn around.

"Yeah?" I mumble.

"Wes, wake up!"

I can't see anyone. I look around, frowning. "Who is speaking?"

"It's me, Wendy."

Wendy...

Yeah, I know that name. Not as well as Colt's, but it rings like bells, tastes like rain and candy, smells like flowers and laughter.

Wendy.

"Wes, wake up, dammit! Come on, wake up!" Something jolts me, like a gust of wind, the shove of an approaching hurricane. My side hits into something hard, rattling my bones.

I choke.

Can't fucking breathe.

Can't stand upright, my knees can't hold me, and I go down. Roll on my side. Reach for something, anything to hold on to.

"Wes. Open your eyes."

It's hard work. I'm so damn tired all of a sudden. Drained. I reach up blindly and slender fingers twine with mine.

When I finally pry my eyes open, my lids heavier than tombstones, there she is, looking right at me through... the bars of a prison cell? Her small hand is wrapped inside mine, holding on tightly.

"What happened?" I croak and choke again. "What the fuck is this?"

We are in the water. Somewhere deep, judging from the deep blue color, the pressure on my chest. Fish swim around us. I'm… inside a cage? In the sea?

Panic licks at my mind, bites hard, and I jerk, but she's still holding onto my hand, her gaze calm, bluer than the ocean.

"You're okay," she says, and I cling to her voice, her hand, her presence. "It's going to be okay."

"What…?"

"The mermaids got you when the island sank. I came to free you."

Makes sense.

No, wait, it doesn't. But I don't fucking care. She's the answer to all my nightmares, all the despair I've been dragging from the past, all the time I wandered in the dim corridors of my youth.

She came to save me.

And, *hell*, I believe her.

———

She has to release my hand to open the cage and I reluctantly let go. My limbs are like lead. My mind is in shreds.

"Did one of the Reds run me over before the island sank?" I mutter as I drift toward the cage door she's unlatching. "Why the fuck do I feel like roadkill?"

"I have a theory that the mermaids are sucking your life force to sustain their magic," Wendy says, small silvery bubbles escaping her lips. Her long blond hair undulates around her pretty face that's drawn in lines of concentration as she works the heavy latch. "Something to do with Peter."

"Peter? Where is he?"

"I don't know. Haven't found him yet." She slowly pulls the

door open, gives me an expectant look. "Where are the others? Did you see where they put them? Do you remember now?"

"Wendy..." I float out and draw her into my arms, kiss her lips.

"Wes." With a small sob, she kisses me back, throwing her arms around my neck. Salt and sweetness and oh yeah, it's all coming back to me.

I pull back. "The others. Colt and Tink."

"That's right. They went down with you when the island collapsed, I..." She looks away, swallows. "I saw all three of you go over, fall into the sea. And now, today, passing over in the boat, I saw all three of you from above, in these cages, so you see I know..." Another hard swallow. "I know they must be around here."

I have so many damn questions crowding my head.

Like, what boat? How did she get here? How are we breathing underwater? Why aren't we dead? What is the meaning of all this? Why isn't there a clean ending? Why cling to hope?

And what the hell are we supposed to do now?

I thought once the island fell, our fight would be over. Our struggle ended. The war on the island, the war to save both worlds, concluded and done with.

And yet here we are, at the bottom of the ocean.

Wendy says she'll save us, but how?

"Come on." She reaches out her hand and I take it again in mine, pushing off the ground to swim out of the cage.

Turning my head, I take my first look at the prison that held me, where I drifted in my worst memories, take in the height of it, the shiny bars, untouched by algae and corals. Like a tower it rises over me, like a rocket about to fly off into space.

Other cages stand all around us, similar to mine, and people float inside, faces slack, eyes closed or half-open. Blank.

Light dances over the cages, over their tall bars and grid-like domed roofs, the prisoners' hair dancing with the sea currents, clothes flapping gently around them.

It's damn creepy.

It's fucked-up, is what it is.

Wendy tugs on my hand and I turn back toward her. She gestures at the other cages and I shake my head. I have no goddamn idea where the others are.

"They have to be close by," she says, more tiny bubbles escaping her mouth. "I saw all of you from above, your cages grouped together."

Resisting the urge to kiss her mouth again, to push her against a cage and press my body to hers, feel her solidity, her beautiful curves, to convince myself she's back and she's real, I accept that with a nod.

Kicking my legs, I swim between the towering cages, tugging her along, the situation finally sinking in, urgency gripping me. Wendy is right, these cages are sucking something out of us, our life energy, killing us slowly. I need to get everyone out.

First, I spot Colt.

I release Wendy's hand to grab the bars. He's floating close to the top of the cage, arms loose at his sides, dark hair weaving around his face.

"Was that how I looked?" I whisper, shocked. "Like he's..."

Dead.

"Yeah. I'll open the door." She kicks her legs a little and slides to the other side of the cage while I stare at my other half, my not-brother, my mirror image, gripping the bars so hard my knuckles go white.

"Colt!" I shake the bars. They are solid, not giving an inch. "Colt, wake up! It's Wes. Come on, man, wake the hell up!"

Reaching between the bars, I grab his arm, shake it.

His eyes fly open and he jerks like an insect caught in a web.

He blinks at me, his gaze dazed and confused. "What the hell?" he mutters, bubbles escaping his lips.

It makes me fucking grin. "Wakey, wakey. I think you got enough beauty sleep, don't you?"

"Are you drunk?" He passes a hand over his face, then scowls. "What the fuck, Wes, am I in the water? Is this a fucking prank? Did Tink put you up to it?"

"No prank, man."

He grabs the bars, presses his face between them. "Fuck."

"I know." I press my forehead to his.

"I was wandering the world alone, looking for you, but I couldn't fucking find you, or the others, and—"

"I *know*." I pull back. "Look, Wendy is opening the door for you. Come on out, we got work to do."

"Work?"

"Need to find Tink, Peter and Jas. Come on, move your ass."

Wendy pulls the door of the cage open, and with one last questioning glance at me, Colt moves toward it.

"Find them?" He takes Wendy's hand and swims out of the cage. "What happened, you lost them? Misplaced them?"

"We'll freshen up your memory," Wendy says. "But first, let's find Tink."

10

WENDY

We swim further, Colt on one side of me, Wes on the other. Both are frowning, handsome faces set in harsh lines. They're also both holding my hands, pulling me along in ringing silence.

"It was the mermaids, wasn't it?" Colt says after a while. His dark hair flows about his head like a thundercloud. "The island sank, we fell into the sea... and the mermaids caught us."

"Give the man a prize," Wes mutters, as if he hadn't been just as confused when I got him out of the cage.

"And Peter?" Colt asks. "Where is he?"

"I don't think he's in a cage," I say.

"Why not? Because he's a king?"

"Because I didn't see him in the cages when I looked down from the boat," I mutter.

"And you recognized us from seeing the top of our heads?" Wes wonders with a chuckle. "What the fuck?"

He's right and yet... "I did see you," I whisper. "I don't know how."

"Well," Colt says pensively, tugging on my hand, "you have special powers in this world. It's your world, after all."

"I thought the island was my world. Not the rest of it."

"Unless a part of the island is still standing and we are in its waters."

Cold shudders through me. "There's still a small island standing. A rock, really."

"That would explain it," Wes says.

"The bridge is still standing," Colt breathes. "All these centuries, all this struggle, and it didn't work."

"But I faced my fears," I protest. "Which is why the island sank. I don't know—"

"You do know," Colt growls, not glancing at me. "Bridges such as this one are built from people's dreams. Certain people have more powerful dreams than others. More painful. With deeper roots. People like Peter."

"...what?"

"And people like you."

"What are you saying about Peter? He was like me?"

"Most probably. Hard to tell after all this time, and with everything that went down. Whether he built part of the initial island." Colt huffs, releasing a string of silver bubbles. "Whether he caused this bridge between nightmares and reality. One thing is for sure. This place changed him, this shadow was torn, and the divinity got ahold of him for good."

"What divinity?" I kick with my feet to avoid getting dragged behind them, my hands almost slipping from their hold. "And I don't understand... I thought Peter came here of his own free will."

"Oh yeah. When home is hell, you'd run anywhere to escape," Wes says darkly. "And he found his way here. He found Hook here. And his curse became his mission, to find the right Wendy, save or sink the island. Save the worlds and himself in the process. The Lost Boys drifted here, too, for similar reasons. The island turning us mad, one after another, year after year."

I frown. "I'm not mad—"

"Whoever comes to Neverland goes mad and dies, Wendy. Unless they are magical themselves or are turned into a magical being, like Peter was. I remember it all, now." Wes is quiet for a long while. Then he says, "Colt, are you going to ask, or should I?"

"I'll ask," Colt says, slowing down, turning his face toward me. "Is Jas here?"

I stare into his dark eyes. "Yes. He found me in the human world. Helped me return."

"Well, I'll be damned," Wes says. "Jas wasn't joking when he said he's on our side? The fuck."

"Saving your asses time and again didn't register, huh?" I sigh.

"Wait," Colt says, "he's the one who brought you back? What the hell? He shouldn't have. He should have left you there, where you were safe!"

"And left you to die?" I demand, indignant. "Besides, he didn't want me to come. I insisted."

"You..." Colt shakes his head at me, brows drawn together. "Don't you get it? It's—"

Wes yanks on my hand, stopping us, and speaks just one word. "Tink."

———

TINK IS FLOATING INSIDE A CAGE THAT GLIMMERS LIKE SILVER AND crystal, pink and copper hair rippling about his pale face, his tattered white T-shirt billowing about him.

One of his wrists is tied to the bars with a silver chain.

"Whoa. What's going on here?" Colt grabs the bars of the cage and hisses, letting go. "They burn."

"They are afraid of his magic," Wes says. "I wonder if he woke up and fought them once already, making them wary of him. I wouldn't put it past him. He's like a feral cat."

But we have found him, and now my worry has shifted fully to Peter and Jas. They must be kept at the palace. The need to see them, touch them, make sure they are okay is eating at me.

"Tink." Wes reaches carefully between the bars to touch him and jerks. "Ow. His skin is burning, too."

"He's glowing," Colt breathes. "Like a sun god."

The shadow of wings behind him, he glimmers in the blue water, a halo around his head. Floating there, he does look like a young god, bringing light to a dark age.

"Tink!" I yell. "Tink, wake up!"

"Tinker, wake up, dammit." Wes braves the burn and grabs Tink's arm through the bars, shakes it. "Hey, Tinker Bell. Wake the fuck up! You're being sucked dry by the merfolk, buddy. Come on, open your pretty eyes. Fucker, can you hear me?"

"Better hurry up," Colt says.

I turn to him. "What? Why?"

He points off to the side.

Mermaids. They're swimming toward us, a swarm of snake-like movement.

"Oh, just great," Wes growls, shaking Tink's arm some more. "Tinker, goddammit!"

Sparks fly and suddenly Wes tumbles backward through the water. I make a grab for him, catch his leg and drag him back toward us.

His hair looks frazzled. His eyes are wide. "He zapped me!"

Colt starts to laugh.

But at least Tink's green eyes are open, and the sparks fizzle out and die as he blinks and takes us in. "You. Wendy."

"Hi, we exist, too," Wes mutters, straightening. "Do you remember us? Your brothers in arms? Your—"

"Oh, fuck." Tink looks past us, eyes going round, and that reminds me of the approaching mermaids. "I don't care what the fuck happened, just get me the hell out of here."

Using the bars to pull myself along, I rush around to the

cage door and put my hands on the lock. A small cry escapes me. It burns like fire, so I release it. "Burns! What should I do?"

"It's your world," Wes says, "remember?"

"So what?"

"So make it not burn," he says.

Make it not burn.

"Hurry up, girl!" Colt is looking in the direction from which the shimmer of mermaids is coming—and they do seem to shimmer as they glide through the water, moving like iridescent streaks of light. "They're almost on top of us."

Make it not burn, Dee. Come on. I draw a deep breath. *It doesn't burn. It doesn't burn. This is my dream, my nightmare and I want to open this goddamn lock!*

Open!

And the lock shatters, its pieces falling softly through the water, a gentle explosion that sends various schools of small and larger fish scattering.

Tink shoves against the bars of the cage, sinking down and kicking the door open.

"Let's go!" he says and we don't need to be told twice.

When he catches my hand, I smile at him, getting an answering flash in return, and then we're swimming away, weaving among the cages, Colt and Wes hot on our heels.

"Peter?" Tink asks, pulling me along so fast the cages are becoming a blur. "Where is he?"

"Probably the palace. No idea, really. And Jas—"

"*Jas* is here?"

"He was going to dive in and get you out," I say, a little defensively, "but the mermaids pulled him out of the boat. So I dived after him."

"You? You dived voluntarily? Weren't you deathly afraid of the sea?"

"Still am."

"Color me impressed," he breathes.

"You should be." I shake my head. "I still can't believe I did it."

He grins, another sharp flash of white teeth. "I *am* impressed, princess, I *am*. Now let's go grab Peter and Jas and get out of this fishbowl."

That's the plan.

———

"Have we lost them?" I wheeze. If this is a dream, then it feels damn real.

"The mermaids?" Tink snorts a stream of bubbles, tucks me into his side as he slices through the water, pulling me along. "They're probably waiting for us to swim right into their hands."

"Reassuring." I huff. "And you seem awfully calm. You don't even wonder how we are breathing underwater?"

We finally clear the forest of cages and the palace rises before us, turrets made of coral lace and domes covered in anemones, with groves of green sea grass flanking it.

"*You* are doing that," Tink says. "You make sure we're breathing underwater And being in that cage, used as a living battery for the fucking mermaids... it jostled my memory some more. You know how Peter has been losing his memory here. Mine—ours—isn't faring all that great, either. It's the effect of this place that's out of time."

"What did you remember?"

"Everything," he says quietly. "At least, everything I knew. And it isn't good."

I consider that. "You mean, about your past?"

"Of sorts."

"Can't you just speak plainly for once?" I roll my eyes. "We're at the bottom of the ocean, about to take on the entire nation of frigging mermaids. Talk."

"Not the entire nation," he says. "Just this one city."

"Oh, right, that will make *all* the difference when it comes to them against the four of us."

"We're not just any four people," Tink says, setting his jaw as we head for the gates.

He's right. We're not, are we?

As Colt and Wes come to flank us, as the massive gates of the spiraling, octopus-like palace rise in front of us, I know it to be true even if I still don't know how it's possible.

"Now what?" Colt mutters. "Do we, kinda, smash through the gates or what? What's the plan here?"

And all three of them turn expectant gazes on me.

"Um. Sure, look to me for ideas," I say. "How about we smash the gates?"

More expectant gazing.

I sigh. "*I'm* supposed to smash the gates, am I?"

"Your world," Wes says.

Right.

Magic them open. Imagine them open. Think of the gates opening and—

A grating sound travels through the water, a deep vibration I feel in my bones before I have even convinced myself to try it.

To try reimagining the world.

The gates sort of... *curl* outward, shriveling like flower petals or leaves, and a procession comes through—mermaids pouring out, and more mermaids chittering behind us, closing in.

Encircling us.

We stop, settling our feet to the sandy bottom of the sea, glance around us.

I squeeze Tink's bigger hand, his long, strong fingers, my breath leaving me in a silver surge of bubbles. "Oh, God..."

Leading them is the Mermaid Queen, her skull-like face making it seem like it's grinning, her long green hair trailing behind her, her powerful tail barely moving as she glides toward us.

She's flanked by two men.

Two familiar, handsome men.

Peter and Jas.

11

WENDY

"What the fuck," Tink whispers, his fingers tightening around mine. "What's going on?"

"They wouldn't change sides," Colt says. "Never gonna believe that."

"They haven't," Wes says. "They're chained."

Now he has said it, I notice the fine silver chains around their necks and wrists and ankles. Thin, glittering chains. They seem decorative rather than imprisoning, though you can never tell for sure. Delicate things are sometimes stronger than steel.

It doesn't help that they're both naked and my gaze skids over sculpted shoulders, arms, chests, down to their legs and their cocks. They're soft, but even so... still impressive.

Mouth-watering. The entire package. Peter and Jas are mirror images of each other much like Colt and Wes are—dark and silvery hair, dark blue and gray eyes, golden and pale skin, both tall, broad-shouldered, and muscular.

And well-hung.

Oh, my...

Stop staring, I tell myself. *Especially not between their legs. Focus, Dee. Dammit, this is serious.*

A constant struggle where these guys are concerned.

"What have we here?" the Queen says, her voice sibilant like a serpent's as she swims closer. Her eyes glow in their deep sockets. "The three *kouroi*. And the girl. Wendy has returned. How interesting."

She doesn't sound interested.

She sounds bored.

Then again, she's a mermaid. Such an alien mind. Such an alien creature. Who knows what she's really thinking.

"I don't see you bowing to your Queen," she goes on.

"We have a king to bow to," Tink says.

"Really? On, you mean *Peter*?" A crackling sound fills my ears. Is that supposed to be laughter? "He's my prisoner. I am your only sovereign now. Bow," she says, "or I'll snap his neck."

"You wouldn't," I say. "He isn't in a cage, and that means you need him for something."

"Wendy, Wendy..." The Queen's long tail curls and uncurls. Her gaze bores into me. "Why aren't you dead like all the previous Wendies?" Her tongue clucks. "No matter, I will take care of it myself."

But before she can move, Tink, Colt and Wes take a step forward, pushing me behind them.

"Hey." I appreciate the gesture—in fact, their instinctive protectiveness warms my heart—but I won't be a spectator. "Guys."

"Stay back, Wendy," Cold says.

When they don't move, I insert myself between Tink and Colt this time and gaze at Peter and Jas. Their faces look kind of blank, which I don't like. "What did you do to them?"

"A jab of mermaid poison," she says and I swear she sounds cheerful. "A bite full of venom."

My chest constricts painfully. "But that will kill them!"

"Will it? How sad." She gives another of those chittering laughs. "You saved them from the poison before, didn't you?"

"Is that what you want from me? To save them?"

"What I want," she says, "is for you to come peacefully with us. Come without a fight, and I will hold my soldiers back."

"Why would you do that?" Tink asks, arching a brow. "If you have the numbers. You know we have the power to annihilate you, don't you?"

"If you try that," she says, "then these two men will go down with me. The chains on them restrain their power. They won't be able to save themselves, and there's also the matter of the poison. It will be time for a new reincarnation but really, do you have the margin for that?"

"Reincarnation?" I breathe. "What is she talking about? Tink, what is she saying?"

"Fuck," Tink says, his face a mask of dread. "The Night of Nights."

"What?" I glance from him to the other guys. "I thought it was already over."

"Because of the sinking of the island?" He snorts. "That was barely a sunset of sunsets. She wants to take over the bridge and for that, she needs a piece of the king."

"A piece?" I repeat dumbly.

"A child," the Queen says slowly, as if that's self-evident. "From the former king," she nods at Peter. "And the new one." She nods at Jas.

"Okay, what?" Wes shakes his head. "Did we know she wanted this?"

"Also that Jas is the current king?" Colt mutters. "Not the best of news."

"Jas is on our side," I say, gritting my teeth. "He cares for you all, so cut him some slack. He didn't choose any of this, same as you."

"Here's where you're wrong," Tink says. "We did choose this, all of us. To escape our pasts. To save the worlds. But there's more at stake here than we ever imagined."

"You know more than you're telling us," Wes accuses.

"And now is not the time to tell you, either," Tink hisses through his teeth.

All of us stare at the Queen and our two guys in her claws, their faces pale, their gazes empty.

"Are you coming?" the Queen eventually says. "Or shall we stand here all day?"

"What say you?" Tink says, glancing at me. "It doesn't seem to me like we have much of a choice. Unless you've mastered your powers yet?"

I shake my head. "I managed to open your cage, somehow, but with them... I don't know what to do. They are poisoned. And chained. And I can't..." I let out a breath, a stream of bubbles. "I don't know how to save them."

"Damn," Colt says.

"Well, until you master your gifts, girl, yeah, no choice," Wes adds. "We won't let them die."

I nod at the Queen. "We'll come without a fight."

"Of course you will," she says. "You're all talk but you don't know what you're doing. Like children let loose in the playground of the universe, aren't you? Guards, bring them in. "

———

LIKE CHILDREN.

She's right.

How the heck am I supposed to save them when I don't understand what I'm doing? It's like... like shooting at a moving target when it's the first time you're holding a gun in your hand. You may get some lucky shots in, hit the target a couple of times, but that doesn't mean you've mastered the art.

And now it looks like I need to master the art ASAP.

No delays.

She tugs on the boys—and it's only then I notice that she's

the one holding the ends of the chains tied around their necks like the leashes of dogs.

It causes a hot well of anger to open up inside of me—and at the same time a different heat spears through me. Why is this strangely hot, that they are leashed like that?

Not for the first time I wonder what is wrong with me.

Way too many things, I imagine. No time to count all the ways I'm screwed in the head right now, though. We follow the Queen and my two poisoned, leashed boys, our two kings-turned-slaves into the palace, through walls that pulse, gelatinous and shot with colors that change.

It's distracting. Even the floor seems to be moving. Breathing. Pulsating.

Fish swim alongside us, sometimes pretty big ones. I don't know how to name them, my interest in the sea and its creatures having died long ago. Their presence makes me shudder and flinch whenever they pass too close.

Guess I don't like fish, slippery and cold and scaly, no matter how I try to face my fears. I don't like being in the sea, with its unpredictable movements and hazards, its currents and fanged monsters.

Maybe my fear of the water is older.

The thought links to an image of my father sitting in the tub, beckoning to me. Pulling me inside with him. Is this...? Is it why...?

The image swirls and fades, though, when we enter a grand hall and I lose the thread.

Like... *whoa*. It's like being on a different planet.

Trunks with branches seem to form the walls, the branches twining overhead to form a dome, but the trees are blue and pink, the spaces in between pale green and violet, light shafting through, shifting on the floor, forming squares and ovals and crisscrossing lines.

It's dizzying and beautiful. Strange and hypnotizing.

Passing under the dome, we find another dilating door that leads us into another similar hall—only this one has a raised platform, pillars placed around it at intervals and colorful strings of pearls and God knows what else hanging between them.

Very festive, whatever it is.

"Is that a giant fucking bed?" Colt mutters. "Son of a bitch."

"A bed?" I blink slowly.

"Baby-making often involves beds," Wes says drily. "Even in the sea, it would seem."

"Fucking hell," Tink breathes.

The Queen yanks on the chains and Peter and Jas stumble against the structure, tumbling down on it, Peter on his stomach, Jas on his back. Water currents lift their hair, tangle and sway it.

"Now what?" I whisper.

The Queen releases the chains and leans back, curling up on the bed beside the boys. "Now you get them aroused."

"Come again?" Tink stills. "You didn't just say—"

"You heard me," she says. "Get them ready for me. They haven't become hard despite my attentions."

"Beats me why," Tink mutters.

I feel sick. I think I might be sick. Can you throw up in the water? This bitch of a mermaid poisoned them and touched them against their will, and now she complains.

Oh my God, I'm going to kill her.

"But you know what," Tink goes on, "though we agreed to come inside the palace without putting up a fight, we didn't agree to take part in your fucking sex games, your mind games, your—"

"Tink," Colt hisses, "shut up." He steps in front of us and bows stiffly from the shoulders. "My Queen. We are at your service."

"What are you doing?" Tink asks, incredulity in his voice. "Colt—"

"Your sexual hang-ups won't get Peter and Jas killed." Colt glares at him over his shoulder. "They are poisoned, remember? We need to make sure they live."

"My *hang-ups*?" Tink splutters.

"Don't pretend not to know what I'm talking about."

"But, Colt…" I start, glancing at Wes and Tink. "Guys?"

"We've come so far," Wes says softly. "And you came to save us. Save us all."

Yes, but getting them aroused for the Queen to use isn't saving them, I think, *not really. It's subjecting them to a new trauma.*

But if we don't, they die, and then that's final. No chance of taking them to the surface again.

No chance of getting them back.

"They're tough," Colt says, as if hearing my thoughts. "They can take it."

Can they? How much can you go through in your life—especially in a life spanning centuries—before your mind breaks? It only takes the last drop, right? The last straw, that's what broke the camel's back. The final stroke.

I think I'm going into shock. With all that happened today, I just… I don't know how to wrap my head around this new development.

But Colt and Wes seem to be onboard. Crazy Twins who aren't really related and yet seem to think so alike. As alike as they look physically, despite the differences in the coloring, their thinking tends to go in the same direction.

I take a step forward and stop beside Tink. Gravity seems to work differently inside this room. We don't float as much, which makes it possible to just walk—light, insubstantial steps like one might take on the moon.

Together we watch as Colt and Wes approach the gigantic bed.

"Undress," the Queen says, waving a hand at them. She just sits there, her fishtail curled, all sagging breasts and rotten skin, skull face grinning, eyes burning, long seaweed-green hair trailing over her thin arms, clinging and winding.

It makes me want to throw up for real.

Colt and Wes exchange a quick look and I can almost feel the internal shrug. Like, why not? No harm no foul.

Peeling off their soaked, half-shredded shirts off their powerful torsos, then shoving down their pants, they end up standing there buck naked and oh my, what a sight that is.

They sort of just tip their heads back, hands held at their sides, facing each other, and I have to tear my gaze off their powerful bodies to look at the rotten Queen and our two handsome Kings on the bed.

Peter and Jas haven't moved much. Jas has only lifted his head, silver hair floating around his face, while Peter has rolled on his side.

"What are you waiting for?" The Queen waves a hand at the Twins. "Kiss. Fondle each other. Put some energy into it. Get on with it."

Colt grabs Wes by the shoulders and slams their mouths together. Wes slides a hand around Colt's neck, gripping it, tilts his head to deepen the kiss, and it's impossible to tell who is in control.

Probably both.

Probably neither.

It's hot. Would have been, had it not been forced on them.

The Queen gives a low rumble that travels through the water, shaking the room. She points a hand a Jas and Peter. "Are you telling me the show isn't enough? I thought you boys were well into one another. What are you looking at?" Slowly she turns her head and stares at me. "I see. You want the girl, too?"

I take a step back. "What?"

"You, girl," the Queen says. "Undress."

Without a word, I reach for the hem of my sweater. I don't mind making out with my boys, even under her gaze. At least it will be for a good cause.

"Join her, fairy boy." The Queen leans back. "You two make out."

I stop and turn to Tink.

Beautiful, he's so beautiful, but the stark fear in his gaze makes my heart bleed. His face has gone white. He talks a good yarn and he's courageous in all the ways that count, but he's not ready for this, and I knew it.

"No," I say. "We won't."

Not like this, not when he still hasn't faced his final fear, in this palace of terror with the weight of responsibility for his friends on top of everything.

"Did you say no?" The mermaid's face twists. She snaps her fingers at Jas and Peter. "Then they will not be allowed to breathe underwater anymore."

And they gasp. Grab their throats, mouths opening, eyes bulging.

Oh, God...

"Wendy," Tink hisses. "Fucking *do* something! Stop her!"

"I told you, I don't know how!" I cry out, frustrated and shaking. "I don't know how to undo her spell."

"Damn," he breathes. "If only we'd had more time, if—"

"You, too, fairy boy," the Queen says and Tink starts to choke.

Oh my God, no. I'm frozen. I try to imagine them breathing but I can hardly breathe myself. Suddenly I'm drowning again, sinking in the deep, unable to draw breath, hands pulling me down to my death.

I'm shaking, shuddering.

Tink grabs my arm. He's trying to say *no* but no sound comes from his mouth. His eyes are wide. His lips form my name. They are turning blue.

"Obey," the Queen says in her sibilant voice, "and I'll let you live."

With shaking hands, I grab the hem of my sweater and pull it up, over my head. I struggle with it and then hands help me get rid of it.

Tink.

He helps me get the damned sweater off, then pushes down my pants, and just like that, we can breathe again. Jas' watch tumbles to the sea floor, and I make a grab for it.

"Leave it," the Queen says. "And take off that acorn from around your neck, too."

My lips pressed together, I do as she bids. *It doesn't matter*, I tell myself. *The shape of things doesn't matter.*

What matters is what is inside your head.

With jerky movements, Tink takes my shoes off and pulls the pants off my legs. His hair has turned black from distress, his eyes a stormy dark gray.

And the Queen is far from done with us. "You, Faery boy. Undress, too. I bet these guys like seeing you naked and getting off. Sex or death. Got it?"

Yeah, that was crystal clear.

PART II

"Just always be waiting for me."
— J.M. Barrie, Peter Pan

12

PETER

The water darkens. It blurs, then clears.

My blood burns in my veins.

Something is fucking wrong, I think, but even that thought is distant.

I'm dead.

Right?

I can't feel my shadow which does point toward being dead but... Should death burn like this? Ache like this? Be fucking agony, making me want to die all over again?

Fuck this.

I'm lying face-down on a soft surface and gritting my teeth, I push with my hands to roll over—only the fire in my blood flares and I groan, only managing to roll onto my side.

Okay, what the hell? What did I miss?

I pat my neck, feeling that a pendant should be hanging there. An acorn... or maybe a thimble.

I frown.

Beside me, on the bed, another body is laid out, a male body, tall and muscular. Pale blond hair, a square jaw... Shit, I know this guy.

"Jas." This makes no fucking sense at all. I'd think it's a dream, only I hurt too damn much. "What are you doing here?"

He turns his head. His hair floats around his angular face. "Take a guess."

"We're in the sea," I whisper.

"You're a genius, you know that, right?"

I ignore his sarcasm as memory returns in bits and pieces. "The island sank. We fell into the sea and the mermaids took us... The Queen took us." I frown at him. "Why would you come here? Are you insane?"

"Me? Did you hit your head?" His face is pale. "I've been trying to save your stupid asses since the dawn of time."

"Always so melodramatic," I mutter.

"Well, for the last couple of centuries at least," he counters.

"You mean, at best."

"Fuck you, Peter."

"Hm." I narrow my eyes at him, deliberately not taking in his naked body. It's been so long but he's hot as ever.

In fact, he somehow looks even better than he had back when we used to fuck like bunnies, back before we tried to kill one another and then remained at war for a couple hundred years.

It has really been too fucking long. Which begs the question...

"Are you telling me that all this fucking time you were on our side?" I ask.

"Yeah."

"So why the hell did you fight us? Why did you become our enemy number one? Why, you asshole?"

His gaze is drawn to something and he replies absently, "Because you were trying to bring Wendy here and sink the island and fucking die, you idiot."

"You didn't want us to die," I whisper as realization dawns.

"That's right. Like I said, you're a fucking genius. Only took you an eternity and a near-death experience to figure it out."

"You didn't want us to die and that's why you made war on us," I say slowly, ignoring his sarcasm.

"Ah-huh."

I wave a hand at him. "Instead of just... you know. Telling us."

"Uh."

"Jas, goddammit, look at me!"

"Fuck, are you seeing what I am seeing?" He rolls on his side, too, facing me. "What in the fucking fires of hell is going on?"

Right. I can see now why he's distracted. I mean... the sight of Colt and Wes naked is hot.

The sight of the grotesque Mermaid Queen curled up on the edge of the bed between us is not. In fact, it makes me cold.

My body doesn't know which way it's supposed to go. My dick is very fucking confused.

Though the strange fire in my blood might have something to do with it. My vision is slightly blurry. I shake my head to clear my sight but it starts a pounding headache behind my eyes.

Dammit.

Behind the Twins that aren't twins, I blearily make out two more people standing and... *Tink.*

Yeah, I know the shape of the man. Definitely him.

And a girl. Pretty. Blond. Nice curves. I kind of know her shape, too, very pleasing shape, sexy, and I...

Oh, what in the fuckity fuck? *Wendy?* What is she doing here? And ah fuck, I sensed her earlier, didn't I? Why do I feel like I'm drunk?

A terrible suspicion enters my sluggish, fuzzy mind. "Jas, is this your doing? Did you go and bring her back?"

"She made her choice," he says. "I couldn't stop her."

That makes me laugh, and ow, my chest hurts.

"Pay attention," the Queen snaps at me. "They're putting a whole show on for you and you're laughing? Shut your mouth and watch."

I gape at her, my laughter turned into wheezing. She's holding three items in her hand. A golden acorn, a silver thimble, a crocodile-skin waist watch.

This is all wrong.

And then memory returns in sharp fragments and… *the Queen wants a child with me. With both me and Jas.*

Fucking hell.

As in, no way in fucking hell. Ever. Nope. *Niet.*

But then Wes slides his hand around Colt's neck, pulling him in, and they kiss.

Well, kissing is too mild a word for it, I guess. They really go for it, groaning as they eat out each other's mouths, and fuck, that's damn fucking sexy.

So sexy, and yet my dick is still acting confused, half-heartedly trying to stir and failing.

Glancing sideways at Jas, I find a frown on his face and a similar situation down below. Of course, my gaze snags on his cock and his balls and his muscular thighs, and well, damn. By all rights, my cock should be hard as a pole by now.

And then I glance back at the guys who are still kissing and now also groping each other, and behind them Wendy and Tink that I'm dying to get my hands on, and goddammit, how is it possible to have in front of me all the people I crave and not even get half-hard?

Colt pulls back from Wes, still holding him in his arms, and glares at the Queen. "How do you expect them to get it up, when they are poisoned? Give them the antidote."

Poisoned.

Oh right. Nice. Now I get it. The strange feeling is starting to make sense, the strange fire in my veins is explained. Not drunk, just... you know. *Dying.*

Jas looks murderous. Then again, Jas often does. Either calm or ragey. That's always been his MO.

A crazy bastard, like the rest of us.

He used to fit right in before he started his personal crusade to stop us from bringing Wendy over and fixing or sinking the island. For a long time, in my defense, I had hoped that Wendy could just fix things. Save the island. Save us.

But you can't make an omelet without breaking eggs, can you? That should have been my first clue.

Jas knew it all along.

Cocky bastard.

And...

"...Dammit, Pete, stop spacing out on me, will you?" Jas has turned his murderous gaze on me. "She poisoned us. A lethal bite. She's not playing around. We have to move from here—"

"Shut up," the Queen hisses, turning her skull face to glower at us, and damn if the cold doesn't seep deeper into my bones.

"You're more insane than I am," I whisper, impressed.

She regards me for a long moment like I'm an amoeba in her soup. Do mermaids eat soups? Probably not. My brain feels scrambled. "Is it true that the venom won't let you get an erection?

Oh yeah, I must be hallucinating, to be having such a conversation with the Mermaid Queen, but... "For sure. Fucking dying doesn't help me get fucking aroused."

Her features relax and I swear now she looks amused.

Can a skull look amused?

"The antidote," she says, "is in my saliva. Come get it."

Wait... what?

Jas growls like a caged animal. "You want us to *kiss* you?" he snarls. "I'd rather die."

Kiss her.

Holy fuck.

"Oh, so you want to die?" the Queen asks him. "You want Peter to die? Make your choice, Pale King."

I understand Jas' reaction. Having sex with her feels preferable to kissing. Kissing is... fucking intimate. Sweeter than fucking. You can have sex and never kiss. You kiss and you can fall in love.

Dangerous.

I swore I'd never let anyone use my mouth again.

But God, now I glance at Wendy's blurry outline and wish I had kissed her, kissed her first, before kissing a monster, another monster like me.

Too late now.

Jas moves first, pushing himself to sit upright with a groan, silver hair falling in his eyes. "Let's get it over with."

Dammit, I've missed him, I realize. It hits me like a punch just how much I missed the asshole.

It's like a dream, having him on our side again, having him so near. But I'm constantly distracted—by the scary Queen, the kissing Twins, Wendy, and Tink, so close and yet so far, and the poison coursing through me.

Not to forget, the act about to take place.

The Queen twists around, planting her hands on the bed and leaning toward Jas. I fucking shudder, seeing her from the front, seeing her so close.

A living corpse, a zombie of the sea, her teeth yellow and sharp when she opens her lipless mouth, her eyes burning coals, her hair like snakes.

Normally that would be the moment I'd expect her to eat Jas' face and go for seconds, but he moves first and moves fast.

He grips her shoulder, for support I guess, and goes for it.

Makes my stomach turn.

I get it. Dying now, before getting a chance to touch Wendy and Tink and the Twins would be intolerable. Killing the Queen before getting the fucking antidote would be foolish.

But damn, it burns.

He shoves at her and falls back against the bed what feels like ages later, his mouth and chin smeared with blood.

I like knife play when I fuck, and I have a fixation with blood, a remnant from my fucked-up childhood no doubt—but this feels different.

I play rough but kissing... Dammit, I have a fucking hang-up with kissing.

My mouth has been used in ways that broke me, broke my soul apart before I even stepped foot on the island, and the thought of having it used once more against my will is threatening to break what tenuous grip I have on sanity right now.

No choice, though. She grabs me, hauls me to her, and the air freezes in my lungs. I can't fucking breathe.

Someone is saying something. It sounds like cursing.

I cling to the sound as she drags me to a kneeling position in front of her. She's taller than me, her emaciated arms strong like the tides. I shove at her and my hands slip on slick skin.

Hell, get on with it, I tell myself. *Do it or die. How's that for an incentive for your very first kiss?*

So I kiss her, press my mouth to hers, but her tongue slips between my lips, cold and slimy and I fucking gag, bile rising in my throat. Her teeth sink into my lips, the side of my mouth, pinpricks of pain.

It galvanizes me. With a growl, I shove again, and this time I manage to break her grip on me and her liplock.

With the back of my hand, I wipe the blood oozing from my

mouth, glaring at her as I fall back on my ass on the bed, trying to ignore the sick racing of my heart. "Fuck!"

But my head is starting to clear, so there is that. Not poisoned anymore. Back in the game.

With the clearer head comes the realization that we aren't just underwater but in the ocean, in the Mermaid Queen's palace, in her room, on her bed—and memories.

So many goddamn memories that remained buried deep for so long. I pass a finger over the scars marking my inner arms and shudder.

What is this? Some kind of reverse magic? Is getting poisoned and then revived such a good jumpstart for one's mind?

"You faced a fear," Jas says, and fuck, I hadn't realized I'd been speaking out loud whatever thought popped into my head.

Real clever, Peter.

Also, fuck this. "Why aren't we out of here already?"

"Because of the guards," Jas says, nodding at two doors on either end of the room where mermaids are lurking. "We are inside the palace, my friend. Think they'll just let us walk out?"

"Fuck. True."

And there is Wendy...

"You, girl," the Queen says, as if she's heard my thoughts. "Come here. The Fae boy, too."

My vision is clearing and I blink as they walk up to us, hand in hand. Well, Tink has his hand wrapped around hers and it tugging on her a little, but her eyes are wide, fixed on the Queen, which is fucking understandable.

Though mine are fixed on Wendy and Tink because they are naked.

Whoa. I mean, *holy fuck.*

I would still kill for a smoke.

Colt and Wes are standing there, Colt resting a hand on

Wes' shoulder, both bare and fully aroused, big cocks hovering against their muscular stomachs, and now there's Tink all pale skin and lithe muscles, and Wendy, her round tits tipped with rosy, hard nipples, the flare of her hips and thighs, the pale curls between her legs, her small face and those wide blue eyes, like, fuck...

Fuck-me eyes. Fuck-me curves.

I'm getting hard now, slowly but surely, and how. My cock stretches out, rising to point at them, my balls tightening.

"Damn," Jas breathes and reaches down to grab his hard-on.

Yeah.

"Touch her," the Queen says. "Touch them both."

I frown.

"Oh, come. Don't tell me you don't want them?" The Queen harrumphs. "I mean, this girl, you moved earth and sky to get her here. The way you looked at her... Don't you desire her?"

Of course I desire her. This way and every way, and all I want is to throw her down to the rocky ground and take her, here and now.

But then why does something in me rebel? I don't want this monstrous Queen directing us, I want us to be doing this because... we choose to, because we are *choosing* it, all of us, the guys and me and her.

"You, human girl and Fae boy," the Queen snaps. "Get the kings ready for me. I need them very hard to penetrate me." She lifts off the bed with a shove of her hands, her long tail unfurling, beating at the water, sending waves that slam me and Jas backward. She swims just a few feet away to hover as if in the air, watching us with those fiery eyes. "Get to it."

I see the indecision in Wendy's eyes, the flash of panic in Tink's. I wonder if they will obey. I hate to see them forced into this. I fucking hate it.

But I needn't have wondered. They approach the bed and

Wes and Colt do the same, getting onto the soft surface, crawling toward us.

This is happening. Truth is, I'd fucking fantasized about this. Wanted this.

I just never imagined it happening quite this way.

So fucked-up...

13

WENDY

The Queen commands and we obey—all of us naked, bared to her, longing for each other even here, under the sea, in the merfolk's palace. Even in front of her.

It's like a dream, only I know by now not to question the solidity of this place, of this reality.

Of their bodies, so fantastically strong and beautiful, the hard sculpted muscles, the hard lean jaws and hard long cocks.

Perfect.

Calling to me.

Making me forget about the terrible Queen watching us, hovering in the water on the side like an angel of death, and feel the fire in my belly, the ache deep inside of me where I need them. My breasts feel heavy, my nipples taut and aching.

Despite my fear, despite my rage, I've never been more aroused.

All of these guys, every single one of them, attracts me, has a sexual pull on me that echoes deeper, somewhere in my heart, doubling the effect, sending it back redoubled until I can't breathe with my need for them.

Skin on skin. No, *more*. Skin on skin won't be enough. I need them inside of me. I need all of them to touch me, hold me, bruise me, sink inside of me.

I crawl over the bed to reach Peter and Jas. They're painfully hard, their eyes trained on me as I approach—on my swaying breasts, on my floating hair.

They both reach for me and I let them grab me, drag me against them. They press me between them and I gasp at the feel of their naked flesh against me—hard muscle sheathed in smooth silk, hard cocks rubbing over my skin as they close in on me.

"Wendy," Peter whispers, trailing his mouth over my neck, his hand coming up to cup my neck, and I whimper at the familiarity of the gesture, the excitement of it, while Jas presses his chest to my back and slides his hands into my hair, pulling my head back.

"The Fae boy," says the Queen, her voice like grinding rocks. "I said he's to join in."

"No," Peter says, pulling back from me, a dark scowl on his face, the ink on his skin barely visible, pulsing like veins. "Not Tink. You can make us do whatever you want. Not him."

"Is that so?" The Queen lifts a hand and Tink grunts, hands going to his throat. "Are you sure we have to go through this again?"

"Dammit," Jas breathes.

She's just cruel, a real sadist, taking pleasure in our suffering. I wonder if she has it in for Tink in particular— maybe because he's kin of hers, Fae blood running in his veins, as in hers.

"Decide," she says, flicking her fingers, and Tink starts choking again, his cheeks flushing, body spasming. He goes to his knees in the water, though they never quite hit the floor. I go down with him, cupping his face, weeping tears that merge with the sea.

Frustration wells up in me.

Let him breathe, I think, *let him breathe!* But fear is clogging my own throat and I can't remember how I helped them in the past. How did I cure him from the poison? Why can't I recall? Am I suffering from the same memory loss that affects Peter?

"Stop this!" I shout at the Queen. "Stop it!"

Peter's eyes are wild. Jas looks pissed. The Twins kneel down beside Tink and shake him as if that can help him breathe.

"Now," the Queen says, and gestures with her other hand, "like I said. The Fae boy. Get on there. They are all looking at you like you're the kind of candy they never tried."

Tink gasps, slumping between the Twins and against me, hauling in great gulps of—water, not air, but it seems to do the trick. He shivers in my arms but his breathing is easing out again.

He's okay.

Damn her.

I turn toward him as he stumbles toward the bed, helped along by Colt and Wes whose faces are like thunderclouds. They're protective of Tink. Always have been.

Of him and me.

When I reach for Tink, I find myself smiling, a bittersweet thing. I feel an affinity with him that I don't feel with the others.

It's not a stronger feeling, just a different one. The dynamic is slightly different. Tink can still overwhelm me, do what he wills with me. He's as tall and probably as strong as the others, and let's not even mention his magic—but he's also somehow more vulnerable than them and has a darkness in his past that matches mine.

His breathing is shaky as he climbs onto the bed, and I'm not sure whether it's from the choking fit the Queen caused or because of what is going on and what is clearly expected of him.

Still, he smiles at me, a faint curve of lips, and takes me into his arms.

He's always been more relaxed around me, kissing me, touching me, something I've never seen him do with the boys.

At least there is that. And true enough, he seems to search my mouth willingly for a kiss, sighing against my lips.

"Wendy," he whispers against my mouth. "Listen to me. Every dream begins with a dreamer. And while in every dream there is a nightmare, in every nightmare there is also a dream."

"What does that mean? What am I supposed to do?"

"Dream," he says. "Dream of something better."

"You think it's that easy?" I hiss, drawing back. "Think I haven't tried? Just rearrange reality, a snap-your-fingers-and-make-a-wish sort of thing?"

"No, not like that," he says, urgency stark in his eyes. "You have to see this world for what it is."

"And what would that be?"

His lips trace my jaw, then press to my temple. "A construct. A puzzle. Small pieces you can rearrange. Look beyond the surface to see the parts that compose it. Realize that not all of them are set. That many of them are movable."

"And how am I supposed to tell the movable from the unmovable ones?" I whisper. "How about *you* do something? What about *your* magic?"

"All gone," he grinds out. "All sucked out of me."

Holy crap.

"Stop talking," the Queen says, "and get on with it. My patience has its limits."

"You've done it before," Tink tells me, ignoring her.

"Not consciously. Not purposefully. I don't know how I did it."

"It's your dream!" Tink hisses, gripping my shoulders hard. "Your nightmare and your memories are shaping this place."

"That's not helping!"

"Focus on what was important to you. Scary to you. Those are the main components you brought with you. Face your fears and change the world."

"Guards!" The Queen lifts a hand and they swarm inside the room, mermen and mermaids with wicked tridents in their hands.

Shit. "Tink... I'm sorry."

"Don't be. If you were hurt and can still do this," Tink breathes, his handsome face grim, "if you find pleasure in it... then I should try. I can't let my fears control me. You shouldn't be the only one to face her past."

He makes me want to cry.

"Hey, chin up." He touches my face. "I like you. I want you. That was never the issue, so... this should work."

"Tink..."

"I more than like you, Wendy. I think I love you but..." His voice cracks. "I've never fucked a woman before. Never done this for the pleasure of it before."

Jesus.

I'm sure I'm crying again but my tears melt into the salty water of the ocean. "You shouldn't be forced to do this."

And yet it seems he does, that he has to face his fears here and now and make out with me, with us, at the Queen's command.

"The Twins," the Queen says, directing us like a puppet master, pulling our strings. "I want them on the bed with you."

"What in the fucking hell," Colt mutters but climbs on behind Tink gamely, Wes following close behind. "What do you want from us?"

"To see some action," she says. "Haven't seen much yet in the ways humans arouse each other. I want the Twins on the Fae boy while he fucks the girl."

"What?" Tink glances back at her. "What the fuck."

I sigh. Caress his face, his high cheekbones, his square jaw.

"Just play along," I whisper. "Hopefully we don't have to go through with it."

He nods, molds his body to mine and kisses me again. This kiss... it's nothing like the kisses from before, the ones we shared on the island. Those were hard and violent, fueled by anger and despair.

These are soft and sweet and unexpected. They grip my heart and *twist*.

Sweet and hot, they make me throw my arms around his neck and press my breasts to his hard chest, scoot closer until I can fully push myself against him until I feel him hardening, I feel a moan rumble in his chest. He's losing himself in it, in me, forgetting to be afraid, erasing the past to feel and enjoy.

But then he jerks, gasps, and I see the Twins behind him. They are touching him, as the Queen instructed, running their hands over him, and the calm seeps out of him.

He pulls back, breathing hard. His face is pale, clammy. "Stop, fucking stop!" He whirls about, lashing at the Twins, shoving them off him. "Don't fucking touch me."

"Tink." Wes looks pained. "We'd never hurt you."

"Fuck," he breathes. "I... fucking can't."

"Are we back to that?" The Queen leans forward, her green hair writhing around her face. "I might kill him this time, let you play with his corpse."

"You can't hurt Tink!" I plead. "Please. Leave him out of this."

Her skull face shifts minutely. "Guards! It's time to make them obey."

14

WENDY

The guards swim toward us, raising their tridents. Wes cries out when one of them prods him with it and clasps a hand to his arm. Crimson spreads in the water.

"Stop it!" I shout. "Stop! Don't hurt them."

Another guard prods Peter. More crimson spreads. His tattoos writhe but his shadow doesn't rear up behind him like it used to. Is it the poison? Is it something else?

"No," I whisper, "please, stop this."

"All that because the Fae boy won't play?" the Queen says, her voice rising. "Humans make no sense.

"You don't understand," I say.

"Don't I?" The skull's eyes turn to me. "Oh, I see. You volunteer, then?"

I swallow hard. "Volunteer for what?"

"To take his place. Spread yourself for them."

"I..." *Come on, Dee, say it. For Tink.* "I do. I volunteer."

I'm not sure but I think the skull grins. "Then let me see you do it. Spread."

"What do you mean?"

She leans forward. "I'll spell it out for you. Get on all fours.

Hand between your legs. Spread yourself. Let all of them have you."

Jesus.

But better this than the alternative, than letting Tink take the brunt of this punishment.

Swallowing hard, I get on all fours. I'm certainly no blushing virgin and here, in Neverland, I've given into my fantasies and desires with abandon. I've felt guilt sometimes, true, and shame for the violence I enjoyed, but I'm coming to terms with all that. I like what I like, and these boys are giving me exactly what I need, so why feel any shame? We're all consenting adults.

But this... feels like more. Exposing myself not only to the boys but also to her and her guards. Being made to do it, just like she was trying to force Tink.

For the boys, I think. *For me. Forget about the others. Do it for the boys.*

So I slide my hand between my legs and spread the lips of my pussy, as my mouth trembles and my core clenches. A strange feeling fills me. Not shame. Not embarrassment.

It feels more like liberation.

Like acceptance.

With a helping of anger and defiance.

"Fuck," Peter breathes. "Would you look at that? You're beautiful, Wendy."

"Magnificent," Jas agrees.

The Twins and Tink are grunting, and turning my head I see them all stroking their cocks that stand rigid and flushed against their muscled stomachs, their eyes dark and fixed between my legs.

It makes my insides tighten as if I'm about to come just from their gazes on me.

Then Peter groans, a deep sound that pushes into me, and I'm coming, moaning and shaking.

Good God...

After a long moment, I realize the Queen is quiet. Is she also looking at me? I can't see her from this angle.

"Do you want us to fuck *her*," Jas says mildly after a while, though his voice is wheezy, "or *you*, Queen of the Sea? Make up your mind because this is getting a tad confusing."

"You're a pervert, aren't you, majesty?" Wes grinds out. "You want to watch, is what this is all about?"

"She's pushing us to our limits," Peter says. "Maybe it's not a child she wants but our madness."

"I thought we were already there."

I remove my hand from between my legs and sit back, turning to look at the Queen who has risen from her throne, still trembling from my release.

She's glowering at them. "The more you push back, the more I will demand."

"No," I start, "please—"

"And I demand that you take two in one hole," she says and gestures at the boys. "Go on. Do it."

Peter groans. I'm not sure if it's pain or arousal but his cock is hard and flushed purple, so I guess it's the latter.

Yeah, he does seem to like the idea, but...

"No," I say, "I can't. I don't think I can."

"I don't care what you think you can or can't." The guards move in on us, sharp teeth bared. "Sex or death. Can't see where the snag is. Surely you prefer pleasure to agony."

I'm panting. I want them to use me. But the boys hold back.

"Not like this," Peter says. "Fuck, not like this."

"First, I want to watch you debase yourselves," the Queen says, her face writhing. "Force yourselves to do things you don't want to do, for all the time you spent thwarting me. This is for my own personal enjoyment. And then... Then I'll have what I want from the two kings. I'll take it from them."

"That sounds a lot like rape," I breathe.

"Isn't that what they did to you?" she sneers. "All those times on the island?"

"Never." I lift my chin, let her see the truth on my face. "I wanted it. And they knew it, every single time."

"Even when you were scared to death? I could taste your fear in the air."

I shiver knowing she possesses such a power. "Even then."

She gazes at me with that unfathomable dark gaze. "Well, one way or another I will get what I want. And it's fun watching you all writhe in agony first."

Yeah. No surprise there. Her taste for the pain of others is obvious. So different from my boys who want to see me enjoy it, enjoy their blend of violence and pleasure.

All she wants is pain.

One of the guards lifts a trident and jabs at Colt's back. He jolts forward with a hiss.

"Fine," I say.

A silence spreads, rippling in the water.

"Wendy," Peter starts.

"I said fine." I don't lift my chin, don't challenge the queen, not to give her any pretext to hurt my lovers more, but I'm telling her the truth.

I have accepted what I like, what arouses me, that I want all of my men, that I want them to push me to the edge of pain and pleasure. And it means I can take control, be the one in charge.

"You don't want this," Colt starts.

"Who says I don't?" I say.

"If it's to satisfy her—"

"How about this being about satisfying me?" I whisper. "Who will take up the challenge?"

Tink is watching me with wide eyes. The others with raised brows.

The queen's tail lashes at the water.

"Holy fuck," Jas groans, "you are serious."

"I'll do it," Peter says and my heart gives a throb I feel between my legs.

I knew he'd be in. But who else? I glance around at their handsome faces. My bet is on Jas, but before he opens his mouth, Wes beats him to it.

"I volunteer."

I didn't quite expect that but why not?

A sound ripples around us. Maybe it's the queen laughing. Maybe the ocean is boiling. I don't care.

This is about taking back control, taking back my life, owning up to all that excites me, all that I repressed for so long.

This is who I am. No excuses necessary.

And then they are on me, tumbling me down on the bed, and I let it happen. Let my body take over as they press their muscular bodies to mine, as Peter hauls me against his chest and Wes molds himself to my back, his teeth grazing the side of my neck, making me shudder.

The world fades as Peter runs a big hand up my side, over my breasts and higher, to curl around my neck, pressing lightly into my windpipe. I'm not breathing air but the act itself makes me clench and whine with arousal.

Wes slides one hand around me to stroke my pussy, setting arousal spiraling through me, setting my blood on fire.

"Yes..." I rock back against his questing finger, hiss when it breaches me, massaging me inside. "Wes..."

Meanwhile, Peter's mouth trails over the side of my neck, sharp teeth sinking into my earlobe, stinging my sensitive skin, fanning the flames.

Wes' hard cock presses against the small of my back, thick and hot. Peter's cock slides against my stomach, between my breasts, a burning snake, long and rock-hard.

The anticipation is killing me, the thought of having both of them inside me making me dizzy.

When Peter's hand slips off my neck and down my body, his

questing fingers, long and strong and clever, joining Wes' inside me, I moan and tremble.

They fill me and scissor their fingers to stretch me, and I'm impatient for their cocks. I don't care who is watching and why, but I do feel the eyes of my men on me, glimpse them at the periphery of my vision—Cold, Jas, and Tink—and it makes me feel like I'm a queen.

The queen of the world.

"Please," I writhe under the onslaught as their hands move, fingers thrusting in and out, their hot mouths warming my neck as they hunch over me. "Do it now. I need it, I need you both inside me…"

Wes groans my name and guides his cock between my legs from behind, sliding it back and forth over my folds.

Peter is still fingerfucking me but an answering groan rumbles against my neck. "Woman," he whispers. "What you do to me…"

His fingers withdraw just in time for the head of Wes' tip to slip into me. I gasp as the broad head breaches me. He pushes me forward, against Peter as he thrusts deeper into me. Peter catches me, leaning back, his eyes dark with desire as he supports me, letting Wes mount me.

"Fuck," Wes breathes against my hair, his hips jerking forward, driving his cock inside me all the way, until his balls slap my flesh. "Oh fuck…"

Peter is shuddering, his hands sliding to my hips, holding me in place. His cock bumps against my belly, trapped between us. His mouth slants against my temple, against my cheek, never meeting my mouth.

"Peter," I gasp. "Want you…"

With a soft curse, he frees one of his hands to grab his cock and point it at my already full pussy. The head of his erection nudges at my stuffed entrance, stealing my breath. Wes grunts and grips my waist hard enough to bruise, hissing when Peter's cock pushes in.

My mouth opens but no sound comes out. I fall against him, against his hard chest, clutching at him as he inexorably drives his cock into me, inch by broad inch, alongside Wes', spreading me so wide I can't breathe.

"Oh shit," I think as now both their cocks fill me, still pushing into me.

It hurts.

It's too much, I can't take them both. I scratch at Peter's chest, my eyes stinging, my tears mingling with the salty water. I'm swimming in a sea of tears, a sea of my own choosing, a pain I wanted to experience.

I'm sobbing, my confidence that I could do this shredded, my body a vessel of pain, and I don't know how to deal with it. It wasn't as I imagined, I didn't want this—

"Take it," Peter rasps, "take it all. Good girl."

"Ours," Wes growls in my ear, "you're ours. Open up for us, Wendy."

Something changes deep inside me. I relax, tense muscles unclenching, and they slip inside, so deep inside I think my soul is pierced.

Too much and yet perfect, too big and yet just right, the sensation riding on the sharp edge of pain and yet amazing.

The best.

Oh my God...

It doesn't take Peter's mouth on my breasts or Wes' hands on my ass to get me off. It doesn't take them playing with my clit or thrusting hard and fast inside me.

The moment stretches, the throbbing of their cocks thundering through me, a flood rising, a swollen river breaking its banks.

Grabbing me and hauling me for the ride, kicking and screaming.

I do scream as I come, caught by surprise, caught by the

violence of my release, feeling as if my body is shattering, coming apart in a slow explosion, filling the dark water with stars.

"Holy fuck," Wes groans, his cock jerking as he starts coming, too. "Peter—"

"Stop," the Mermaid Queen says. "Pull out."

"Hell," Peter hisses. "Just let me... come, you bitch, I..."

A guard hauls Peter away from me, his cock dragging as it slips free in degrees, my clenching pussy refusing to let go.

I cry out in shock, Wes clutching me, his cock slipping out, too. The pain is bigger than it should be, as if something in my mind has torn.

"Now come, King," the Queen says, "and put your seed in me."

"No." I'm breathless, still reeling as the guard drags a struggling Peter toward her, my thoughts a distant buzzing. "Stop!" Anger is filling my chest. Rage. "Enough. You can't do this."

The queen roars. "And there you go again, challenging me." She lifts a hand and points it at me. "Enough with you."

"No—"

Her face transforms, twisting into a snake's, or a dragon's, hard to tell. She opens her mouth and a terrible scream tears through the water, making us all groan.

And my lungs spasm, my ability to breathe underwater failing. I grab my throat, gasping, choking.

No.

Predictable but effective, her way of shutting us up. Unless she got fed up with this game and decided to kill us all off.

Not letting it happen.

"You can't." I scowl. "My world. My rules. We can breathe just fine underwater."

And my throat relaxes, my choking stops. I breathe in. Moments later my guys close in on either side of me, their scowls matching my own, hands fisted at their sides. Peter is there, too, having shoved the guard away.

"A fluke," the Mermaid Queen says, her hair turning into snakes, mouths snapping in the water. She clicks her tongue. "But did you think it would be that easy? I'll just reactivate the poison in their blood."

"You are a one-trick pony, aren't you?" I mutter, glaring at her.

"They are dying," the Queen says, mouth stretching grotesquely in a parody of a smile. She shakes the magical items she stole from us in her hands. "Only I can save them."

"This is where you're wrong." I can see the poison in their blood, coursing through their veins like bright gold, and I...

I.

Change.

Reality.

I don't just *imagine* a world where Peter and Jas aren't dying of poisoning, but a world where they've *never* been poisoned in the first place. I don't imagine, in fact, I *will* it. It is the way I know it.

"Done," I whisper.

Peter and Jas glance at each other, then turn wide eyes on me.

"I felt that," Peter says. "Everything shifted."

Jas is rubbing at his chest. "Such a fucking weird feeling."

"You did it," Tink whispers, still pale but a smile tugging at his lips. "You did it, girl. We're getting out of here."

The Twins grin widely, mirror images of each other.

I open my hands palms up, and the items the Queen has been holding onto—the acorn, the thimble and the watch—materialize there.

I clutch them,

"What did you do?" The Queen glares. "What do you think you're doing?"

"We won," I say.

"What nonsense. How are you thinking of winning this battle?" the Queen says. "There are six of you and an army of us. A nation of us, waiting to be called from the deep."

"But we have her," Tink says.

"The girl?" The Queen titters and chitters in laughter. "Just because she pulled a couple of tricks you think she can save you?"

"She is the *Kore*," Tink says, a satisfied smirk on his face. "She is awoken."

15

COLT

In a daze, I watch as Tink climbs off the massive bed and stands in front of the Mermaid Queen. He's a strong one, Tinker, probably the strongest of us, though he's also the prettiest of us. He's no delicate flower.

And he knows things, things hidden from the rest of us. Always has. Probably what gave him that sarcastic streak he flaunts about.

That, and his past, a past he's never talked about but of which we have caught glimpses over our long years together.

Though his last comment...

"Who is this *Kore*?" I mutter.

Peter blinks. "What are you saying, Tink?"

Jas sits up, a frown on his face. "No way."

Wes grunts a curse when the mermaid turns her full attention on Tink, but instead of going for him, as I thought, Wes grabs Wendy and hauls her to him.

"We should get going," he says.

I blink. I'm still hard, still all worked-up, still fully fucking confused. "What just happened? Did Wendy do something?"

"Yeah, dumbass. She really did." Peter grabs Jas by the arm

and Wendy by the hand and starts moving toward the bed's edge, too. "She's getting the hang of it."

"The hang of what? Changing the world?"

"It's called Self-realization," Jas says, his speech a little slurred, as if he's drunk.

"Is it, now?"

"Maybe." He shrugs, grunts as he swings his legs off the bed and shakes Peter's grip off. "She's realizing the truth of this world, which is her dream world, and that she has a great power over it. A power she never grasped before."

"Sounds like voodoo," I mutter. "Or yoga."

"Those two are not the same thing," Wes says, frowning as he helps Wendy off the bed. As if he has ever studied either voodoo or yoga, that fucker. "Hey, Tink!"

Wendy shakes Wes' hold off her, too. She hangs the magical items around her neck, clipping the watch together with the acorn on the same chain, her small face set in thoughtful lines. Her expression is so intense I can't look away, even though she's standing in front of me naked and hot, her breasts so round and perfect, her hips made for my hands.

Can't look away except when I realize that everything is frozen—the guards, even the Queen.

"Are you doing this, Wendy?" I hop off the bed, reach for her. "Fuck, Wendy..."

She shudders, takes a stumbling step back and I steady her. "Tink?"

"Yeah, let's grab that fucker, too." I take hold of his shoulder, jerk him backward. "Tinker, come on, man. Time to hit the road. Or the sea paths. Whatever."

"The Kore," he whispers, staggering sideways. "The Kore, the Underworld, the currents of fate..."

"Stop mumbling and get moving."

"The gods," he says, his eyes unfocused as he turns toward me. "Castor."

Castor.

The word—the name?—hits me like a fucking punch to the stomach and I groan, doubling over. "Tink…"

"What's going on? What does it mean?" Wendy puts her arms around me. "What is that?"

"Pollux." Tink glances over at the others, points at Wes. "Pollux, hear me. The wheel has turned."

"Christ's sake, is he an oracle now?" Wes mutters and grabs me, hauls me against his side. "Let's get going before this spell breaks. It's our only chance."

"What is Tink talking about?" I breathe as he pulls me and Wendy through the room. "And wait, what about him? And the others?"

"They're coming."

I crane my neck and manage to see Peter pulling both Jas and Tink along through the rows of guards who seem frozen—floating in the water, still, so still they might as well be statues.

How does it work? How can they hover in the water without moving?

Her world, I think. *Self-realization* or whatever this shit's called.

It doesn't have to make sense to me. It does to her. It's her dream. She's controlling it.

"Couldn't you just, I dunno, imagine us on the surface?" I mutter. "Huh, Wendy? Or on a nice tropical island, in a hammock with coconuts and cocktails?"

"Stop your muttering," Wes says, "and help me figure out which way to go. Wendy, do you know?"

"Wendy, are you all right?" I reach for her across Wes' back, my fingertips brushing over her skin. "Say something."

"You're right," she says, "I should have imagined us on the surface, I just…" She closes her eyes. "I'm scared to make it worse instead of better. It's still my nightmare, you know."

"Fuck. I'm sorry. How can we make it better, girl?"

"Keep moving," Wes says, "keep mov—"

The guards burst into motion, coming after us—maybe it's guards who weren't in the room with us before, since we're now clearing the grand doors we went through earlier, but what do I know—and the time for thinking and wondering is over.

"Goddammit!" I start to swim, doing my best to increase our speed. "Come on."

But Wendy is sluggish, her hair tangling in front of her face. A thin trail of blood floats around her face.

Something's wrong.

Shoving Wes to the side, I lift her in my arms and do my best to move forward. Her eyes are kinda glazed and the blood is coming from the corner of her mouth. "Talk to me, Wendy. You okay?"

"The gods," she whispers.

"Forget about the gods. Don't pay attention to Tink, he's a crazy bastard."

"The Underworld," she goes on. "And Gorgon."

"Wendy..." I'm lagging behind. Peter and the others are catching up with us already. Wes stops, turns around, beckons frantically for me to move faster. "Can you stop the mermaids? Freeze them. Like you did inside the palace."

She breathes more words but I can't make them out, red bubbles escaping her lips. Her lashes lower, her body going slack in mine.

"Wendy!" I shake her. "Wake up!"

"What's going on?" Jas asks, swimming around me to touch her face. "Is she all right?"

"How the fuck should I know?" I snap.

"Wendy!" Tink shoves Jas away and cups her face. "Take us out of here. Wendy!"

She moans a little, lashes fluttering. "Out?"

"Out of the ocean. You can do it. Your dream, Wendy, remember? Come on!"

We're all gathered around her now, every one of us guys touching a part of her, our hands on her legs, her arms, her neck, her belly. All gazing at her and wanting her and hoping, even as the mermaid army bears down on us.

Fucking crazy.

And yet I can't bring myself to protest or say anything at all.

It's all brought us to this moment—my past of growing up with Wes, of being separated for what felt like forever, of finding Peter and his rugged bunch of Lost Boys, of having Wes join us, of finding friendship and love, trust and lust—fighting for a cause together—then finding Wendy, the island collapsing...

It was meant to be, somehow.

This is the moment that will decide it all. But I already know it was worth it, for me. No matter what. Just being here with her, with them, it's all I've ever wanted.

She stirs in my arms, blinks up at me, her gaze finding each one of us and lingering for a moment. She smiles.

And we're yanked upward, gasping as an invisible force drags us through the column of water, up and up, surging through schools of silver fish and blooms of golden jellyfish, through swarms of slippery eels and floats of tunas and sharks.

We burst through the glittery surface and splash around, gasping, cursing. Trying to breathe, to gather our pieces back together.

She pulled us out of the depths.

She got us out.

It's finally sinking in. We escaped.

"This is what I'm talking about!" I mutter, swirling Wendy around in the churning water, suddenly exhilarated, improbably hopeful. "You got this, girl!"

She laughs, too, and although there's still blood trickling out the corner of her mouth, she looks better than she had in the deep. Less pale. More alive.

I turn her around once more, just to hear her laugh, and in every direction, I see water and more water and…

"Where's the island?" I ask.

"Focus, Colt," Wes says. "The island is gone."

"Right. *Fuck*." I clutch her to me. "I forgot about that."

"Not all gone," Jas says and points.

I turn in that direction and squint. "What, that rock? That's what's left of it?"

"And that's a lot." Jas nods at our girl in my arms. "She hasn't faced her final fear, which is why it's still standing. A work half-done at best."

Well, that's a buzzkill.

No island and also no full destruction of the bridge between the worlds. Looks like a botched mission, any way you look at it.

Not her fault.

No, it's ours. We heaped too much on her. Forgot that, magic or not, she's only human.

"We need to get out of the water," Peter says. "Before the mermaids come for us and drag us back down."

"Small goals," I mutter, gazing down at her, my heart curling with warmth for her, "right, girl? The King is right. Let's get out of here, and then we can see about that last fear of yours."

She presses her lips together and nods.

That's my girl.

Our girl.

She's in my arms now, and I focus on that, a moment of bliss in this fucked-up life, as I swim toward the shore.

16

WENDY

We're swimming toward the island.

Well, Colt is swimming, carrying me in his arms. The magical tokens are burning against my collarbone, the chains chafing around my neck.

I guess I could just... teleport us there or something. Magic us on the shore. I don't even know why I'm clinging to the pendants, as if they can help with something.

See, I still don't have a good grip on how to do this. It's like... learning to ride a bike for the first time and you keep falling, and you know you have understood the principles of it but you need practice to maintain balance and keep going.

Still, though... I think of the sea as a flat mirror, smoothing out the waves. I think of a net underneath us, protecting us from the mermaids coming to get us.

I think of the island as having a wide, sandy beach that makes it easy to get out.

And there it is. A white beach, turning the rock into a tropical paradise.

Colt grins at the sight of it as he pulls me toward it. "That's sweet of you, woman. You heard my request."

Well, the beach may look tropical but the rest of the island is still a standing rock. Should I make it prettier? I'm so frigging exhausted, I loll in Colt's arms.

It's as if their touch, their naked bodies, their hands trailing over me, their attention and focus on me have unlocked my mind, but my mind is tired and would like a break to regroup and take stock of the situation.

We're in this middle world, surrounded by Faerie and the ocean with its murderous merfolk, stuck on a rock standing in treacherous waters, and there's been talk about having to sink this rock and face my final fear—not necessarily in that order.

I can hardly think about that, though, as we approach the beach. Too tired. I fight Colt until he relaxes his hold on me because he looks exhausted himself, his handsome face drawn, eyes bloodshot.

Once he lets go, I do my best to swim alongside him, not even having the energy to marvel at the fact that I'm in the sea and not freaking out.

Freaking out is *so* yesterday's news.

Today, I can move in the water and shift reality and be with my men.

If only I didn't feel like I'm about to pass out.

In the end, Colt and Wes end up dragging me up onto the white sand, and we all drop there, panting and groaning, six bodies washed out of the ocean.

But we're out of the water. I'll take that as our first win. Surviving the island's collapse, the Mermaid Queen's malice, the merfolk guards coming after us, the rolling waves.

The water itself.

I'm spitting salt and sand, panting, unable to get enough air into my lungs, and my five guys heave and curse as they struggle to get their breath back.

We're all naked, limbs covered in white shell fragments, and

I'm still holding onto Colt, but I also reach for Peter who's stretched out beside me, needing to touch them.

"Wendy..." Wes puts a hand on my ankle. "Are you okay?"

"I'm fine. You?"

"I'm okay," he rasps. "Tink?"

"Mfmf." Tink rolls on his back, spitting out sand, letting his arms flop by his head. "Yah, okay. I feel like someone sucked my blood out. I didn't know we had vampires around here. What gives?"

"The Queen almost sucked all life out of you," I whisper. "There are so many cages down there. We should—"

"Slow down, girl," Colt says, sitting up with a groan. "Let us catch our breath, first. Jas, you all right? You're awfully quiet."

"Alive and kicking." Jas sits up, too, shoving pale hair out of his eyes. "Well... alive, at least."

"Guys... we're out," Peter says, lifting dark lashes to gaze at me. "We made it out. Wendy saved us."

And suddenly I find myself inside a knot of sandy, muscular bodies, crushed half to death and yet... and yet oddly touched and pleased as I put my arms around my guys. I didn't expect this group hug from them and my heart feels full.

"I'm so glad you guys are all right," I whisper, tears clogging my voice. Happy tears, tears of relief, of suppressed worry and stress and panic.

"You came back for us," Tink says and there's awe in his voice. "For *us*."

"Hard to believe," Colt says, his voice low and raspy. "No other girl ever even liked us."

"They all went mad," Wes breathes.

"With good reason," Peter says, muffled.

"That's because they weren't the right ones for us," Jas mutters.

"I'm the right one for you," I say and I feel the *rightness* of it in my bones. "I was made for you."

"I think *we* were made for you." Peter pulls back to meet my gaze with his own. "Made for you and waiting for you through time."

"Peter." I slide my hand around his neck, pull myself closer to him. "It was your acorn that brought me back."

"No," Jas says, "I told you before, it wasn't. Magic helps but it was your desire to save them that returned you, girl. To save all of us. The acorn was only a focus point."

"Don't diss the magic, it works," Peter says but he's grinning. "Your thimble," he pats my pendant hanging at his neck, "was all that kept me from going insane since the island collapsed."

I stare at it. Then down at myself, at the golden acorn gleaming against my collarbone. When I glance sideways at Jas, I see his watch in his hand. When did that happen?

"Then you're better off than the rest of us," Colt mutters, kissing my neck, distracting me.

"Hear, hear," Tink says, rubbing his cheek on my arm.

"Oh, come on, are you claiming to be sane, Peter?" Wes chuckles. "You're kidding us."

"We like you that way, though," Colt says. "We're all crazy here. You'd stand out too much if you weren't the same."

I turn in the circle of their bodies and touch each one in turn, smiling at them, and on their exhausted, drawn faces, faint smiles form in reply. They are genuinely happy I came back for them, and it makes me stupidly happy in return.

"We should make a shelter," Jas says, "before night falls."

I lift a hand to his face. "Why, does anything live on the island?"

"No, but mermaids can crawl up beaches just like we have. We need a safe place to rest, somewhere they can't get to us as we sleep."

"Fuck, he's right," Colt says. "What if they come up to us and drag us away as we dream—"

"Stop," I say. "This is my fear, not yours."

A ripple of silence spreads.

"The mermaids? Not too sure about your theory," Wes says. "I hate mermaids. And clowns."

"Me too," Colt says.

"It doesn't matter. I was afraid of water." I consider that. "I still am. But it's not a crippling fear anymore."

"So what does that mean?" Jas whispers, taking my hand off his cheek and kissing my palm. "What are you saying, Wendy?"

"I don't know. But I won't let them get to us."

Jas tangles our fingers together. "What are you going to do? Lift the island higher? Build a wall around it? Turn the sea into a desert?"

"Will there be camels?" Tink says. "I've never seen a camel."

"No camels," I say, smiling. "Sorry, Tink."

He shrugs. "Ah well, what can you do? Pity, though. I've always wanted to travel. Too late now."

"It's never too late," I tell him determinedly.

He sighs. Pushes copper and pink strands out of his eyes. "Wendy..."

"Just wait." I dive deep into my mind, into myself, and think of a world where the mermaids are cute and peaceful and small like little fish.

Little cutey fishies.

Singing trilling little songs.

"What are you doing?" I distantly hear Wes asking. "What is she doing?"

Tiny mermaids that sing to the moon and curl up on rocks, and frolic together in the waves. This is going to be fun.

I open my eyes and squeal.

"What did you do, Wendy?" Colt comes to take my other hand, his dark eyes serious. "You changed something important, didn't you?"

"You can say that again." I smile at him. "Suffice to say you needn't build a fortress to sleep in. There's no more danger from the sea. Well, apart from sharks and rogue killer whales, of course."

"Are you serious right now?" Tink's green eyes are wide. "Did you imprison the mermaids? Did you kill them all?"

"I didn't kill them," I say.

"Did you build a giant cage for them underwater?" He twines a finger in my hair, tugs lightly. "That would be poetic justice. Or a giant... a giant bubble made of glass to keep them inside?"

A cage. That reminds me... I think of the cages under the sea, and I think of them dissolving. I think of a great ship coming to rescue those still alive.

But my guys don't know what I'm doing, so I turn to them. "Let's see where we can sleep tonight. I trust you to keep me warm."

That earns me five sexy grins.

"You can count on it." Wes bows in front of me. "Shall we, my lady?"

————

WE SLOWLY PICK OURSELVES UP FROM THE BEACH AND MAKE FOR the rocky rise up ahead. Jas seems to have a plan, so we're letting him pull us along. His hand is crushing mine and I welcome the small discomfort.

The sun is dipping over the horizon, turning the sky and the water red.

It looks so much like blood, I shudder.

Jas is leading us uphill, a determined look on his face, fair hair plastered to his temples and neck. It's such a desolate place, this rock in the ocean.

But I can't imagine rebuilding the island, bringing it back. It feels... wrong somehow to change this remaining balding rock with its scraggly trees and bare stone.

Not sure yet what that means and why.

Dragging our feet, we climb up to the summit of the rock and descend to the other side where Jas claims there's a cave we can fit into. He's the only one who has explored the island so far, so there's that, my brief stay notwithstanding.

A salty, cold breeze blows in from the sea and the sage bushes and lone trees creak and sigh. I should be freezing my ass off, but with the guys around me, I'm kind of protected from the elements.

Or maybe it's just that I'm kind of lost inside my own head right now, until Peter grips my left wrist, hard—the feeling comforting and familiar—stops.

"Here, is that a ship I spy?" He gazes out at the sea. "Or am I hallucinating?"

"It is a ship." Jas stops, too, squeezing my hand. "Where did she come from?"

"The Fae shores?" Wes hazards. "Looks like a Fae ship. Best keep your heads down. We don't want them seeing us. The Fae king is a nasty sort, or so Tink says, right, Tinker? Dear old daddy is an asshole."

Tink stares at the ship. "They are hauling something out of the sea. Nets?"

"Doesn't look like nets," Colt says. "Traps?"

"That big?"

"Shark traps?"

"Shut up, you idiot," Jas says. "It's the cages."

A hush falls.

"Oh fuck… Wendy." Peter lets out a wheezy chuckle, jerking me by his grip on my wrist closer to him. "Is this your doing?"

They all turn to look at me, questions in their eyes.

"It is my nightmare," I say, my face warming, tugging my hand free of Jas's hold to regain feeling in my fingers, "and therefore my fault those people were trapped. So I imagined them getting rescued. I thought up a ship to rescue them. We couldn't leave them there to rot."

"And the mermaids?" Colt asks. "Won't they hinder the rescue efforts? It's their prisoners, after all."

I glance at him, grin a little. "No. They won't."

He doesn't ask me why. His gaze is back on the ship, thoughtful.

"Well, I have to say." Peter finally relinquishes his hold on my bruised wrist to sling a muscular arm around me. "You rock, woman. I always knew it."

That makes me laugh and I stop myself from calling him out on his bullshit. "You're not too bad yourself."

"You only say that because I saved you all those years back from drowning," he says.

"So you remember it now. Tell me what you remember."

"One day while stalking the beach where your family had taken you on a boat ride, a small bay with a pier, islets and rocks, I saw you fall into the water. Nobody else had been around—it was winter and the place was remote. I dived into the sea without a second thought, swimming faster than I ever have in my life. As I approached, I could see the boat drifting away, your parents yelling at each other, your brothers cowering. I dived deep and pulled you out, shook you until you coughed out an ocean of water.

My eyes burn. "Peter... I never thanked you properly for it."

"You'll get a chance to thank me properly." He wags his dark brows. "I'll make sure of it."

It makes me laugh some more.

He has changed, I think. He looks more relaxed. Calm. Doesn't have that wild look in his eyes anymore, the one that said he clung to sanity by a fraying thread.

The smirk he gives me is lazy and sharp and full of dark promises. It makes me gulp, starts a throb between my legs.

"Shelter," Jas says, clapping Peter's back. "Sleep. Rest. Sex later."

"Maybe for you, old man," Peter says. "We young people can get it up without getting our eight hours of sleep."

But he's bluffing because once we get going, it becomes obvious they're all at the end of their energy reserves.

And so am I.

"Let's go before it gets dark," Jas says. "Come on, the cave isn't far."

He keeps forgetting I could change night to day, this rock to blooming fields, so he's going on as if reality is fixed, as if one has to accept it.

And he's not the only one who keeps forgetting it, fighting it.

I do, too.

Enough.

17

WENDY

The cave is just a rocky overhang over a basaltic floor, dark and damp and pretty much exposed to the wind from the sea. It's the best this island has to offer right now and obviously better than sleeping in the open, but...

Enough. Enough fighting it, Dee.

My head or my heart may be telling me I shouldn't return the island to what it was before, but nothing is being said about this cave.

Nothing is being said about making something new.

The guys are already exploring the so-called cave, muttering curses and trying to think of ways to make it more comfortable for sleeping.

Tink is swaying on his feet, and the Twins are not much better. Peter and Jas are the only ones still going, clearing the area of dead branches and a few rodent corpses.

Jas says something about using the branches to create a sort of wall on one side, block out some of the wind.

"Guys," I say, "stop."

They pause and glance at me. I feel their eyes on me, weighing, expectant.

But my gaze is on the cave. I look at it and think, there's no cave there but a *house*, a white *bungalow*, with *palm trees* growing in the front and *hammocks* hanging between them.

Rose bushes grow in the front in a garden overlooking the ocean, their scent wafting on the breeze, and sturdy pines on either side of the house cut off the cold wind.

I set a table with chairs there, too.

The sight of the ocean doesn't scare me anymore. It's peaceful. And this is my view.

"Holy shit," Peter breathes. "Now, this is what I'm talking about."

"Hammocks!" Wes makes his way to one of them, runs a hand over it. "I've always wanted to have a hammock. Colt, get in here."

Colt hurries over and they fight to both get into the same hammock.

Jas shakes his head and chuckles. "Boys."

It's as if they're reclaiming their lost childhood, the innocence and playfulness they didn't get to explore when they were young.

It makes my eyes fill up even as I smile.

"Wendy," Tink says and comes to take my hand, grinning. "I see you're getting the hang of it."

"Better late than never, huh?" I smile at him. "God, Tink, you look beat."

"Why, thanks." He laughs quietly. "So do you."

"Flatterer."

"Is there a bed?" he asks. "That's all I need."

"A huge one," I say. "And the pantry is full. We can eat something before turning in."

They gather around me again, the house and the hammocks all forgotten, their eyes bright.

"You're a little wizard," Jas says.

"Or a witch," I say.

They grin and laugh and I've never seen them act so much like little boys before but when they jump onto the bed and roll on it, well...

It makes me so glad. So glad I can do this for them, for us. As long as they return to their sexy adult self later.

It's about time things took a turn for the better.

———

"I LIKE IT," PETER DECLARES, BELTING THE COBALT VELVET ROBE around his lean hips.

"You do?"

"Ah-huh." He juts his chin toward the others who are similarly getting into robes of various colors I thought up and laid on the white corner sofa. "I like these robes. Easy to get into, easy to get out of." He wags his brows.

This new, teasing Peter keeps making me laugh.

"Like yours," he goes on, stepping closer to me, grabbing the tassels of the belt of my light pink robe—because why not pink, right? I deserve some pink after all the black—and pulls me to him. "So easy to take off..."

Oh yeah, these aren't little boys, not at all. Though that playfulness lingers, and it makes me so glad.

"There are sandwiches in the fridge!" Colt shouts from the kitchen at the back. "Come get them!"

"There is a fridge?" Peter hauls me against him and grins down at me. "For real?"

"Pastrami sandwiches, man." Wes has joined his brother in raiding the kitchen. "And fruit! And booze!"

"Holy shit." Peter's grin widens and he turns his head, effectively distracted. "Is there any Gin?"

I think of Gin, *think* it into reality, and Colt laughs from the kitchen. "Yeah. Got some Gin. Come in here."

"In a moment," Peter says, his gaze finding me again. "You shouldn't spoil us like this."

"Why not?" I stick my tongue out at him. "You deserve to be spoiled. And we all deserve a little celebration."

"When I found you..." Peter lifts a hand to trace my mouth, his eyes softening. "I never expected all this. Never expected you."

"Makes two of us," I whisper. "But I don't regret any of it."

"Neither do I." I gaze into his bright eyes and feel like my heart is about to burst.

"I'm starving," Wes declares, coming out of the kitchen loaded with food. "Shall we sit outside?"

"You just want to eat while swinging in the hammock." Colt follows him, carrying at least a dozen bottles in his arms.

"Why not?" Wes says.

Right, why not? I follow the Twins with my eyes to the door and out, as they head toward the hanging hammocks, while Tink appears, carrying a tray with sandwiches and a big smile on his face.

Aw. Warms my heart to see them happy.

"Coming?" He winks at me, then glances around. "Where's Jas?"

"Out there somewhere," I mutter.

Peter tugs me after him and we come out of the little house to the view of the blue sea. The ship is still somewhere out there, hauling out cage survivors, and the moon is rising.

Jas is standing by the table, arms folded over his chest, head cocked to the side. His robe is a light gray, like his eyes, and it shimmers silver in the moonlight. "What the fuck is that?" he says.

"What's what?" Peter says calmly as we join him.

Tink places his tray on the table and stands beside us. "Music. Voices singing."

"So you can hear it, too," Jas says. "I thought I was hearing things. That would have been worrisome."

"And what the hell is that?" Colt points, getting out of the hammock, a beer bottle in one hand. He uses it to point. "Fish coming to shore?"

Wes has already stuffed half a sandwich inside his mouth and he almost chokes on it as he gets up to look.

We're gazing down at the steep shore below. I didn't think of a beach for this side of the island, so it's just rocks, and creatures are now crawling up and curling on them, small and translucent with rainbows in their long hair.

"The mermaids," I whisper.

"What the fuck did you say? Those aren't mermaids." Colt shakes his head. "No way. Mermaids are fucking scary assholes."

I laugh.

More of the little fishtailed beings drag themselves up on the rocks and trill at the moon.

"Are you serious?" Peter is laughing so hard he can barely get the words out. "You turned our worst enemy into these... pets?"

I shrug, smiling. "It seemed like a good punishment."

"Thou art cruel," Tink says but he's snickering. "It is a fitting punishment indeed. Did you keep the Mermaid Queen as was to witness all this?"

"No, I made all mermaids into these harmless little things," I admit. "I couldn't trust her not to try and hurt us again if I let her remain her true self."

"Good girl. That was wise." Tink comes to take my hand. "I was never much for open endings in movies, because then you always expect the bad guy to come back and bite you in the ass in the sequel."

I snort. "What sort of movies has Peter been bringing you?"

"Terrible ones." Tink brings my hand to his lips, kisses it. "I suppose I didn't like the open endings because I always identified with the bad guys and thought we should go down for good, once and for all."

"And what do you think now?"

His green eyes crinkle at the corners. "I don't know. I'm not used to gray areas. What do you think, Wendy? Are we the bad guys?"

"I don't know who or what you are," I whisper. "But I love you all anyway."

He lowers my hand, his gaze lifting, finding mine. "And if I told you who we really are?"

I stiffen a little, wondering what he's trying to say. "Won't you tell me anyway?"

"Perhaps," he says. "After dinner. I'm famished. After all, does it matter?"

"I guess it doesn't, after all. Because, listen... I lied. I *know* you aren't bad guys, Tink."

"Hold your verdict," he says and I frown at him.

What in the world does he mean?

———

THE LITTLE MERMAIDS SLIP BACK INTO THE WATER WHEN THE moon goes down, tracing bright lines under the surface, and we retrace our steps into the little bungalow. Jas takes my hand, the other claimed by Wes, and the others go ahead and open the double doors to the bedroom.

We haven't been inside the bedroom yet—unless the boys sneaked in earlier, and I wouldn't put it past the Twins, at least, who are curious like cats—but I know what it looks like. After all, it came from my mind, from vague memories of romantic bedrooms I've seen online and in old magazines my mom had lying around.

I'd never pegged myself as a romantic person. Far from it,

and my relationship with these guys sort of proves it, but it fits with this house, this place, this moment.

There's a window with a view of the ocean, long white curtains fluttering, swishing against the walls and the wooden floor. The four-poster bed is enormous, as promised, taking up most of the room, covered in white linen and pale cream and baby blue blankets. Stacks of pillows cover one side.

"You know what I'm gonna do?" Wes lets go of my hand and takes a flying leap into the middle of the bed. He stretches his arms over his head, his light green robe falling open, baring his sculpted body. "Woo!"

"Kids," Tink mutters darkly, his mouth twitching.

"At least I convinced them to wash most of the sand off before getting into their robes earlier," I say.

I laugh when Colt shakes his head, rolls his eyes at Wes—and then follows suit, jumping in beside him and rolling over the covers.

They've never seemed more like twins than they do now. Then again, they did grow up together, a detail I tend to forget.

Then Tink grabs my hand and pulls me onto the bed, too, Jas cursing and chuckling as we topple on top of the covers.

Peter comes to stand in front of us, hands folded over his chest, a frown on his face, but he climbs onto the mattress, too, and we're a tangle of bodies, laughing and muttering and elbowing and kicking each other.

"Covers," Wes says. "Get under the covers. Get in!"

Laughing, we shed our robes, letting them fall over the side of the bed, and drag ourselves up and under the fluffy covers.

I sigh in bliss when the soft fabric slides over my skin, then it gets even better because five warm, strong male bodies press around me, arms winding around my waist, my back, my legs, my head, cradling me.

The guys half-heartedly battle for a spot next to me and I

end up on my side with Peter behind me and Tink facing me, Jas at his back, while the Twins flank us all.

We lie in a heap like a litter of puppies, squirming and hugging each other. Feeling their arms grow heavy over me as they drift off, smelling their male, spicy scent, knowing it's them, that they are here with me, safe and sound and alive, it makes me want to cry with happiness.

It also makes me want to touch them, kiss them, have them, and they also attempt to caress me and get me excited, but we're simply too exhausted for anything but rest.

It's nighttime, the time to slumber and dream, to dream of good things, to set the world to rights again.

As sleep claims me, I think of us together in a future where things are simple and bright, where we can sleep together like this every night and dream together.

———

AND YET I COME AWAKE GASPING, COLD SWEAT DRYING ON MY skin, my heart pounding with fear. What was that?

A nightmare. I rub at my chest. A lingering pain there, though I can't remember the images, only a crushing feeling of dread and... *guilt*?

Not fair.

I did what I could. Faced my fears even if it meant sending the guys to their death, from which they were saved in the nick of time, and I'm still having nightmares?

So not fair.

Face your final fear.

Yes, of course. It's so easy.

I mean, there is a frigging reason I didn't touch these memories in so long. They ache like thorns stuck deep inside my chest, festering, spreading the poison, and though I know that I need to pull them all out, to the very last one, it's so hard.

One last fear...

No. No way. Can't do this now.

I scrub my hands over my eyes.

Outside the window, dawn is breaking, splashing the sky with yellow and orange hues and I've somehow ended up sandwiched between Colt and Jas, their arms heavy over my waist and legs.

Tink has ended up in Peter's arms, Wes holding him from behind. I wonder how grumpy he will be when he wakes up and finds himself in that conundrum.

Or maybe he'll like it, let himself like it. Like me, Tink has been scared for way too long. This is a chance for redemption. For a new start.

Why can't we stay here forever? I don't want to go back. I don't want to go anywhere. Holy crap, I want to remain right here, in this little house on the cliffs with my boys until we all heal.

Disentangling myself from Colt and Jas, which makes them grumble in their sleep and grab for me again and again as I get up, I gather my pink robe from the floor, pull it on and make my way out of the room.

Bathroom pit stop is first, and I take the opportunity to splash my face with cold water, chase the last cobwebs of the nightmare away.

Then I make my way through the sitting room and the kitchen. Dim light seeps through the windows, painting the walls and sparse furniture in pink and gold. I sit down at the long kitchen table and run my hands through my long, tangled hair.

Here, in this house with the view of the distant Fae lands, and the small iridescent mermaids singing to the moon at night, and the rugged landscape.

We can stay here, I think again. We can catch fish and cook them. Hell, I can conjure food, entire banquets. Why shouldn't we take the time to rest and get to know each other, at last?

Don't we deserve it?

Isn't it fair?

Steps echo inside the sitting room and someone appears at the kitchen door, flinging pink and copper hair out of his eyes, broad shoulders bare.

He's completely bare, in fact. Looks like someone doesn't care for the robe I gave them. Not that I can complain when his body is such a work of male perfection.

Tink lifts his gaze and smirks at me, eyes shining. "Here you are."

"I knew you'd run the moment you woke up in someone's arms," I mutter.

He looks surprised. "I... Damn, I did, didn't I? I ran."

"You did."

"It wasn't unpleasant. Just..." Tink comes to stand beside me, a frown on his face. "Not used to it. Not like this, naked in the same bed. So... relaxed."

"I get it."

"I could get used to it," he says, his voice growing quieter as he sets a hand on my shoulder. "I could get used to all this."

"Me too," I whisper back, putting my hand on top of his, craning my neck to look up at him. I smile. "I was thinking just that."

"Well, I was thinking of something else when I saw you leave the bed." His eyes narrow, a predatory grin spreading on his face.

"You were? But..."

Tink steps around me and bends to place his hands on my waist. "I definitely fucking was."

"Tink..."

He lifts me onto the table and I perch on the edge, looking up at him, gripping his corded forearms. His green eyes are creased at the corners, his mouth tilted in a crooked smirk, though there's an uncertain line to his strong jaw. A vein is beating furiously in his neck.

It's easy to be distracted from that, though, by his chest that is like a work of art, brought to life by some long-dead famous sculptor, no doubt, all smooth muscles and hard lines, hard pecs with small hard nipples, a six-pack to die for.

Jesus.

"I want you," he says hoarsely, and I become aware of his cock hardening, pressing between my legs. He grabs my robe, yanks it open, the quick knot I made with the belt loosening and parting.

"Tink…" The golden acorn thumps against my collarbone as he shoves me on my back on the empty tabletop, my head thuds on the wooden surface.

He climbs after me, over me, parts my legs and kneels between them. Runs a finger between my spread thighs, making me shudder. He does it again, parting my folds, pushing his finger into me, and I moan.

It feels so good…

He lifts his finger, sticks it into his mouth, sighs in what looks like pleasure, eyes going heavy-lidded. "Sweet…"

I lift myself on my elbows, open my mouth to speak, but Tink pushes me back down and kisses me hard, pressing his body down on mine. He feels amazing on top of me, tastes even better, like spiced wine, like bitter almonds with a hint of sugar and cinnamon.

Like Christmas and sexy boy.

Like a gift.

A heavy, muscular, sexy gift of a man who grinds his hard cock between my legs, sliding it up and down my seam, making me wetter with every pass. When he finally breaks the kiss, panting, gazing down at me, I almost lose it.

"God, I..." I moan when he reaches between us and rubs against my clit, making me see stars. "Oh..."

So close...

He makes a small frustrated sound when I arch up, a strangled groan leaving his throat, and he abandons my clit to grab his cock and tease my entrance with it.

"Holy crap, I..." I arch again, helplessly, needing him inside of me. *We're really doing this, I think dizzily*, really going to do it. *Tink is going to fuck me.* "I thought you..."

"That I'm broken beyond repair? Feel this?" He pushes into me and I cry out, clutching at his back. "Feel it? Holy fucking hell."

"But in the sea—"

"I was about to do it. Ready for it." He pushes deeper and we both groan. "But the others touched me and it was too much at once, but this..." He thrusts. "This is clear. I want this. I want you. I want... Fuck, I want the guys, too, but I need to push through this goddamn barrier in my head first..."

I take his hand, press it to my breast. "I'll help you."

"You already are, don't you know that? You're saving me." He rocks his hips, thrusts deeper, and we both gasp out loud. "Fuck..."

He grabs my wrists, slams them to the tabletop on either side of me. Dips his head, bites at my mouth, at my neck, sharp teeth stinging, leaving burning marks. Abandoning my wrists, he lifts his hand to one of my breasts and pinches my nipple, hard enough that I cry out.

I writhe under the onslaught. I hadn't expected the pain— but why not? Did I really expect them to become different people? To turn from angry wolves into gentle doves?

His teeth sink into my earlobe and somehow the pain ricochets inside my belly, pooling between my legs, and I clench hard around his cock, so hard I hiss.

And then he bucks and grunts and starts to shudder.

Just as I start to come, shaking underneath him, shaking with the intensity of pleasure that threatens to tear me apart and the knowledge that it was Tink that gave it to me.

Tink overcame his fear and lay with me.

His big cock jerks inside of me as his teeth relinquish their hold on my ear, releasing the tender flesh. He buries his face in the crook of my neck, his hips rocking as he shoots his load deep inside of me.

"Tink..." I breathe as he collapses on top of me, his breath warm against my neck and shoulder.

He's passed out.

18

TINK

Void spreads around me. It's dark but it's also soft and welcoming. There's a soughing sound, like waves crashing on a shore, and a scent of warm skin, spring roses and pretty girl that fills my senses. Her taste is on my tongue, on my lips.

On my mind.

The feel of her wrapped around me, around my body, around my cock, is mindblowing.

I come awake in stages, realizing it's not a dream, and that blows my mind once again, so that I stay still, afraid to break the spell, to find out it's a dream after all, unwilling to shatter the sensation, savoring the feel of her pussy clenched around my still throbbing cock.

I can't have been passed out for long, I think, giving an involuntary shudder and hiss when she clenches again, drawing a spasm from my dick, and I spill some more.

Fuck, so good...

Groaning, I heave myself off her, wincing a little when I see the bite marks on her neck, her ear.

Then I almost fall back down when she lifts a leg and winds

it around mine, drawing my cock in deeper.

"Woman." I thrust once, twice. Goddammit, it's better than any sex memory I have. Makes me want to stay inside of her, keep fucking her. "You're trying to kill me."

She doesn't reply, only moans and grips my arms, pulls me back down to kiss me. I taste blood on her lips. It shouldn't excite me more but it does and I gasp helplessly as I thrust into her again and again.

Another orgasm is tightening its grip on me. I'm Fae, I can fuck all night, but I'm new to this. I've never fucked for the pleasure of it. Haven't fucked in, well, forever, and the intensity is a shock to my system.

My vision grays as she whines, her pussy milking my cock, the pleasure hitting me like an ax blow, felling me.

Fucking hell...

This time I manage not to crash on top of her, catching myself on my elbows. They thump hard on the table and I almost headbutt her.

She laughs breathlessly.

I find an answering grin on my face. We're still rocking together. I lick at her lips, at the blood and her sweetness.

"I hurt you," I whisper.

"Ah-huh."

I grimace. "Fuck, I'm sorry."

"What for?"

"I can't do this gently. Can't love you gently."

"I don't want you to," she says.

"Wendy..."

"I like you the way you are. I swear to God. I like it rough, I like this rough side of you." She strokes the side of my face and her eyes blaze with earnestness. "I like the whole of you."

She truly believes it.

She truly likes me.

Can I trust it? The tangled feelings inside my chest ache

and churn. Sitting back, I pull out of her, breaking the connection—but the feelings remain, making the backs of my fucking eyes sting and burn.

I lift her off the table, in my arms, carry her through the house and outside, onto the terrace overlooking the sea. Striding to the trees, I lie down in a hammock, pulling her to curl against me.

I need time to sort through the thoughts and emotions crowding my head, give them a label, a name. An outlet. I need to talk with the others, be near them, hear how they feel. I have to understand what is going on with me, just in case it all ends soon.

It probably will.

"I know what you're thinking." I stroke her blond hair back from her face. She's curled against me like a kitten, face pensive. "What you were thinking when I walked into the kitchen."

"Do you?"

"Yeah, I do. You were thinking, why not stay here? You can change this world at will. Have feasts prepared. A villa with a giant pool and a jacuzzi. A home movie theater with actual good movies, not the crap Peter always brings me. Tarts and cakes and ice creams. Tame mermaids to eat from your hand."

"Tink..."

"But this is temporary," I tell her as gently as I can manage.

"Why?"

"Because the only reason this rock is standing is that you haven't faced your final fear, and as long as it stands, the worlds are in danger."

She shakes her head, blond hair falling over her eyes. "Forget about my fear. I can't do that. Can't face it."

"Of course you can."

"No." She shakes her head a little. "I won't do that and risk you all dying again. No way. I love you all too much for that."

Love.

The word stops my fucking heart in my chest.

There it is. The name, the label for my feelings. Not that they need one, and it's too many of them—lust, arousal, affection, coziness, ease, fondness, warmth, attachment.

Devotion.

But love... yeah. That covers it, I guess. And fuck if it doesn't scare me all over again. I'm scared shitless to love her. Love them.

You fucking idiot, you always have loved them. You're only just facing it.

Who would have thought that facing your affection and desire for your people would be even more terrifying than facing your fears?

That fear and love could end up being one and the same, that love meant acceptance of the past, of the terror, of the pain, embracing the fear and finding that well of warmth in me once more?

"Tink, are you all right?" she asks softly, her fingertips still tracing my jaw, my neck.

"Yeah," I reply and for the first time I feel it, feel the fucking truth of it, the becoming of it—not all right, not yet, but getting there. "I will be."

I will be all right, fucking all right, even if the end is almost upon us.

———

That's where the others find us soon after. They cast us amused looks but go to fetch breakfast from the kitchen and I haul myself and Wendy out of the hammock to join them at the table on the terrace.

"You look well-fucked," Colt says to me, lifting a brow at Wendy who blushes like a virgin where she's sitting beside me. "The bite marks are impressive."

"They are called hickeys," I inform him. "Educate yourself."

"Aye, aye sir!" He grins and reaches for the ham. "So I shall."

I feel oddly exposed, with all of them knowing I did finally have sex with Wendy, probably wondering if I will also fuck them—which makes me hard and at the same time fucking annoyed—and I have the urge to growl and snap at them.

"Pass me the coffee, will ya?" Peter reaches across the table for the coffee pot and Wendy pushes it toward him. "Thanks, Wendy. So you're the *Kore*, huh?"

Her delicate brows draw together. "Tink said it, not me. I have no clue what he meant."

Oh, yeah. A whole other can of worms, that one. Not one I want to open right now. Not after having her underneath me, and in my arms.

Even if it's exactly what I scolded her for, clinging to his moment, unwilling to face what's coming, despite it all.

But it seems the choice is not mine to make.

"*Kore*," Peter says, frowning darkly. "I know that name. It means the Maiden."

"Maiden?" Wendy glances from him to me. "I think we've established I'm no virgin."

I grin at her, take her hand. "Damn right you're not. Thank fuck."

"The Maiden is an honorific," Jas says. "It has nothing to do with virginity. An honorific title for a powerful woman. There's a story about her..."

"Can't we just have some breakfast in peace?" I snarl.

"Oh, come on, Tinker," Peter says, "this feels important. Tell us what you know."

"Important? Ya think?" I deliberately scrape some butter off the block and smear it over my slice of bread. "But it's a long story and can wait."

"No," Jas says, "it can't. It's time you told us everything, Tink."

"God fucking dammit, I've had my first fuck in fucking ages, and you want to discuss *mythology*?" I get to my feet, pulling Wendy up with me. "Seriously?"

"Woo." Colt applauds, Wes joining in the hand clapping. "Go, Tinker. Lost your maidenhead, did you?"

"I lost that a fucking long time ago," I growl at them and they fall quiet. "But you knew that."

"You know things we don't," Peter says quietly, yet his voice carries over everyone. "We need you to tell us the truth. About who we are. What we are. What this is all about."

"*Goddammit.*" Looks like the discussion can't be put off. I close my eyes, draw a breath. "You know the truth," I say. "You just refuse to look at it, to face it."

"Tell us, Tink," Jas says. "Speak the fucking words."

"You were never human," I tell them, looking at them sitting around the table with the sea rolling behind them. "And you've always known. Wendy and I have been forced to face our fears, guys. How about you own up and do the same?"

19

WENDY

The *Maiden*? What's all this about?

I didn't expect this conversation right now. I barely managed to push my worries to the back of my mind while sleeping with my boys—though they obviously surfaced in my subconscious, in my dreams—and getting fucked on the kitchen table by Tink, at last, had distracted me.

But now everyone is on their feet, glaring at Tink who seems to be all kinds of pissed off.

"You were never human," he says. "You're gods."

"You mean, *we* are gods," Jas says smoothly. "Including you, Tink."

I stare at Jas. Then at Tink. "*Gods*?"

Wait... He's said it before, hasn't he? Something about a thunder god and... can't remember what else. Can it be?

"Talk, dammit," Peter growls.

"And tell you what? Nobody put you here, on the island," Tink spits. "You were here all along."

"This is where you're wrong," Peter says. "Every word I've told you is true, about my childhood, about my past, about my choices."

I shift on my feet and wince. I feel bruised inside but in a good way.

"A reincarnated god," Tink says. "Forced to be born as a human, to be kept away... away from here. But you came back."

Peter's mouth tightens. "I had a war to fight."

He hasn't denied what Tink said, I notice.

A war.

"Jas." Peter is frowning darkly. "Who is Jas?"

Tink shrugs. "Another god."

"Are the Fae involved in this at all?" Wes asks.

"We're gods. We protect all our creatures," Tink says. "Even fallen gods, like us, have a responsibility to all worlds."

"Jesus," I whisper.

"No," Tink says, "actually it's Jupiter. Hence, you know. The name, *Peter*."

I choke a little. "Right. And that makes Jas...?"

"Hades," Peter says, his eyes darkening. "Also called Janus, the two-faced god of fate. Hence, you know. *Jas*. Damn, it's all coming back to me." Peter lets out a breath. "He's the hinge of the world, the revolving door of destiny, and I'm the temple beyond. I am order, he is chaos."

"You couldn't tell from the clothes," Colt mutters. "That he's chaos, I mean. He always looks so well put together."

"You haven't seen him bared." Peter grins, though he looks dazed. "He's magnificent. And his handle—"

"Yeah, okay. So tell us the truth now, Peter." Tink's face is tight, as if preparing for pain, and I know that he loves these guys and especially Peter, so accusing him of something has to hurt. "Did you ever kill someone or was the whole Fae story a ploy?"

"I killed the last king."

"The one who brought the island out of the waves," Jas whispers, "who opened the gates between the worlds and brought disaster. *Cronus*."

"That's another name for Time," Tink says. "What your watch kept record of."

Peter scowls. "This is giving me a fucking headache. The disconnect between the human and other memories is too much."

"And Wendy?" Wes whispers.

Yeah, what about me?

"She has had many names over the centuries," Tink says, not looking at me. His gaze is distant. "Some called her Kore. Some Persephone. She is the one who crosses, the one whose dreams can shape worlds but also kill them. She has always split her time between the human and the otherworld. She is the only one who can cross and live."

"Because she is a goddess," Jas says.

"Because she is the one," Tink says. "Reborn, like we were, in a human body, with a human past, coming back to save us."

"You knew all this?" Wes glares at Tink and thumps his fist on the table. "You had all this goddamn information and never shared it with us?"

"Hold your horses," Tink says. "My memory was affected like yours all these centuries."

"But you knew!" Wes insists.

"Did you know all this, Tink?" I gaze at his handsome face, trying to understand.

"I knew that... something was off." Tink's jaw works. "When Wendy arrived, this Wendy, some of my memories returned, but it wasn't enough. It was bits and pieces. I didn't get the rest of it until she came back this last time. In the cage, I hung there, in darkness, and something switched inside my head, and it all made sense again—"

"Inside your head." Colt taps the side of his own head. "You know what, it all sounds like you made this up."

"Made it up?" Tink gives a dry chuckle. "Are you out of your fucking mind? Why would I?"

"Not on purpose, perhaps," Peter says, "but—"

"Fuck you, Peter." Tink throws himself at Peter across the table and the Twins and Jas get between them, trying to separate them.

I sit back down, dazed. The sea rustles and soughs. My head aches, jammed full of images and strange echoes. "Guys. You know Tink is speaking the truth."

Jas glances at me, still trying to hold Peter back, frowning. "What are you saying, Wendy?"

"Your memories are still muddled," I whisper. "As long as you remain here, in this world, they may never clear completely. But can you honestly tell me that he's wrong? Don't you know who you really are?"

And yeah, I can hardly believe the words coming out of my own mouth, but after everything I've seen, everything I've done... I lift a glass I've pulled out of nothing, out of my head, and look at my reflection, distorted and fuzzy on its curved surface.

Who are you? I ask myself. *Are you a goddess? Are you a force of nature? Are you someone's dream or are you their savior?*

Tink yanks his arms out of the Twins' hold, grumbling something under his breath, and shoves a hand through his hair.

Peter curses and pushes Jas off him.

They're all breathing hard, staring at me, then glancing at each other.

"Shed the glamour," I breathe, putting the glass back down, "shatter the illusion, break the bonds of your minds. Tear down the walls."

I'm not re-imagining the world this time. I'm merely seeing the world as it is, and tearing down the blinders from their eyes, and mine. Pulling down the walls.

I believe them when they say they didn't know.

But now I can see it and I know why I'm here, why I was able to do all I have.

Kore. *Persephone*. It is, after all, my middle name.

Queen of the Night. Queen of Nightmares. Queen of Dreams.

It all makes sense now.

I am the dark—and around me, the world explodes into light.

———

"Whoa…" Peter is staring down at himself. I don't know exactly what he is seeing, but he's glowing, marks writhing on his skin.

Jupiter. Hence, Peter. That makes me snicker. Also known as Thor, God of thunder and lightning. Cloud-gatherer. Eagle-eyed. The Tall Oak. The King of the Skies.

Beside him, Jas looks wreathed in velvet shadows, the paleness of his skin, his eyes, his hair glinting. He is Hades, God of death and the Underworld. The White Snake. The Velvet Poplar. The Cypress Emperor.

The Twins are staring at each other. Snakes seem to twine over them. Dioscuri, twins from different fathers, or so say the myths, born from eggs inseminated by a golden godly rain, one mortal, the other immortal—in the end sharing their immortality. Swan men. Feathered snakes that carry out the will of fate. Soldiers of the divine army.

And Tink, well… he hasn't talked about himself, but he's obviously Apollo, the Archer, God of light and music and dark magic. *Smintheus Loxias*, Killer of the Python dragon, Oracle of the gods, Arrow of destiny.

Faerie is the land of the dead. Neverland is the underworld. The island was a bridge much like Charon's boat on the river of Lethe, ferrying souls.

It's all this, and yet none of it. We are still ourselves, the worlds are still as we knew them. A reality within a reality. A mirror in a mirror.

How do I know these things? Because I am one of them, I am their center, their lover, and the information crowds my head, a throbbing presence.

They stand there, pulsing with power—expressions, manifestations, incarnations of the gods in human form. They are the hands of the gods, the same gods that have been walking among mortals since the dawn of time, changing faces, changing names.

Wind wraps around us, a living ribbon, tying us together, whispering words and names of power. Jas and Peter take my hands, Tink puts his on my waist, gazing into my eyes, the Twins put their hands on my shoulders.

A circle.

And it's not all light and rainbows. The guys' eyes are dark with a black fire, an intensity I feel everywhere, the carnal desire pulsing off them singeing my skin. I can't breathe.

This is us. We've been here before, in other lives, past lives, and now it's going to happen again.

We're going to seal the deal, put our sigil on the magic that brought us here, and I want it. I crave it. I invite the touches on my body, the heat in their gazes.

"Bedroom," I say, just that one word, and the magic flares, making me gasp. The world darkens, too, falls into unexpected night, and if it's at my bidding, I don't even know I'm doing it.

Maybe it isn't me this time. Maybe it's them.

Stars shoot across the sky, exploding like fireworks before they hit the sea, and as the guys lift me between them and carry me into the house, the air glitters, and I see their true faces.

Terrible faces, beautiful and monstrous, skulls showing through the skin, fires burning in the eyes, teeth that are too sharp and long, muscles that are too big for mortal men.

They're gods, and they're just as they're supposed to be.

They're perfect.

To *me*.

They tear the doors of the bedroom off their hinges, smash them under their feet as they thunder into the room. They throw me onto the bed and pounce after me, on top of me, rolling me this way and that to reach me with their hands, their mouths, and then their cocks.

I'm lost in sensation. I wish I could have them one by one, or even three at once, but five is a bit beyond me. We are still human, despite the divine nature showing through, our bodies mortal and limited—and above all my heart and my mind seek out the individual connections.

But right now, I need this.

We all need it.

To connect all in one, to merge and surge together.

It's hard to separate the entities, the godly sparks, as hands spread my legs and fingers burrow inside of me, rough and long, wringing pleasure out of me. I cry out when a hard mouth closes over the tip of one of my breasts, teeth sinking into my nipple.

A jackal-like face leans over me, long yellow canines glinting like knives—and I see Jas' face underneath the skin right before he kisses me—if you can call the brutal assault on my mouth a kiss.

Every small pain, every squeeze and sting takes me higher.

And higher.

When one of them enters me, shoving his cock brutally into me, I almost come. It's Wes kneeling between my legs, grunting as he pushes deeper, and huge wings jut from his back, almost touching the ceiling. Snowy swan wings. He bends over me, his face half-bird half-human, the eyes animal-like, pupils huge, the gold almost yellow, like an eagle's.

And then Colt climbs behind him and from the shout Wes

gives and the widening of his eyes, I know Colt is fucking him in his turn. Colt's wings are black like coal, his eyes a blazing darkness, his face shifting between a monstrous toothed beak and his human handsome face.

Pleasure is a haze, descending over me. I grab onto Wes' shoulders as he fucks me, wondering where Jas is.

But then Peter lifts me to sit and I moan when that forces Wes' cock even deeper. I'm pressed to Wes' chest, my boobs mashed against his hard stomach, and both Twins grunt, leaning back to accommodate me.

I expect Peter to fuck me from behind, but Jas joins him and I gasp when they shove their fingers into my ass.

"What are you doing?" I mumble, then cry out as something huge breaches my backside. Peter is thrusting into my ass—and then another cock joins in and I arch, robbed of breath and speech, a scream building in my chest.

Not sure this is humanly possible.

This could kill me.

But the pain is distant and I'm not fully human, after all. I'm pushed to bend forward, over Wes and Colt who have lain back, as Jas and Peter somehow manage to ram both their cocks into me and start to fuck me like that.

I can't imagine the contortions.

And I don't care.

Wes takes my hands, plants them on his chest, and Colt reaches around Wes to grab my breasts and squeeze, thumping my nipples as I jerk and shake.

Tink. Where's Tink?

He appears beside me, kneeling and parting my lips with this thumb, then straightening and shoving his cock into my mouth—and oh God, oh yes, this is what I want, to be filled and owned and rocked and used, without a chance to think, move, escape or even breathe.

Nailed to the spot, rocked by their thrusts, swallowing the

saltiness leaking from Tink's fat cock, listening to them grunting and groaning and cursing as they take their pleasure with me, I'm so blissed out I start to come without realizing.

Coming apart before I know it, magic and pain and pleasure mingling, exploding, taking me apart molecule by molecule, my scream lost in the din rising inside my head and around me, a whirlwind that breaks down every last wall in my mind, every last vestige erected by magic, and then I fall...

20

PETER

I don't know what the fuck is going on—only that I'm caught in this spinning hurricane of arousal and need and fucking pure lust for her and the guys.

I also know now my true nature, I remembered who I am, who we are.

And if I need blood and pain and pleasure rolled into one giant package with a bow on top, that isn't necessarily divine, but human and just a part of who I have always been.

Still, it connects me to all of them.

We share this need.

We're grunting and fucking and rutting like animals with her in our middle. Pulling on Wendy's long hair with one hand, I grab Jas' head with the other and kiss him hard as we both fuck her ass, while Colt fucks Wes who is fucking her pussy and Tink is fucking her mouth, and she's coming, and I'm coming, and we're all fucking coming, and it goes on and on and it fucking never ends.

We're gods and this is divinity, this animalistic side, this burning chaos.

Men try to behave, to follow norms, they are raised to be

gentle and careful and ethical and good—but gods don't care about that shit, especially among deities. We relish the pain, we relish the loss of control.

It's what makes us feel more like ourselves.

Maybe it's what makes us feel a bit more human, from the days when humanity was as out of control as we are.

Wendy cries out, clenching everywhere, and as if that wasn't enough, Jas bites my lip and pulls, shaking me out of my thoughts. His face keeps going in and out of focus, but his cock is nestled next to mine, shoved into the narrow passage of Wendy's ass, solid as a rock.

He's gasping now, his cock jerking, and he kisses me again as we both shoot our cum, the pressure, the heat, the feel of Wes' cock wedged in her pussy too much to handle.

God... oh, fuck...

Whether I'm a god or not, I feel like I'm wrenched out of my own body when the pleasure slams into me. Knocks me out of my consciousness, so that it's like I'm floating on the ceiling, looking down at the knot of our bodies on the bed.

God of thunder... what the fuck, right? Locked inside me all this time, just for a chance to save the worlds, to shatter this nightmare bridge and safeguard everyone's existence.

World-hopping, plane-shifting to find the one who kept the bridge alive, the one who could kill it.

Persephone, the lady who walks among the dead and the living, lady of memories and dreams, mortal and immortal at once.

Kill the bridge so the souls don't escape, so the living don't stray into the deadlands.

Are the Fae all dead? Are they the souls of the humans who have passed on? Or are they something else? What worlds exactly is this bridge connecting?

I slump over her, Jas slinging an arm around my shoulders, twitching, his pale hair tickling my cheek. I slide my hand over his back to his ass and grab a handful, turning my face to kiss him again.

This is the good life. Getting better and better, godliness or not. This is exactly what I want, what I've always wanted—even if there is no knife play, no blood. This... is stronger than my fixations on violence and the coppery taste of blood. This is fucking *everything*.

Wes groans, muttering some choice curses, and I feel his cock jerk inside Wendy's pussy—the wall separating our cocks is so thin I feel everything, and it makes me moan against Jas' mouth.

Colt hisses something in reply, while Tink gasps and Wendy swallows, the rest of his cum spilling down her tits, over my hand that I have clamped on her waist.

An orgy.

Such a godly thing.

But is it an orgy when you're fucking the people you want to spend a lifetime or two with? When you're spilling your cum inside the woman and the guys you fucking love?

Feels more like an act of love.

———

"Goddamn," Tink grunts sometime later, lying on his back on the bed. "Are gods supposed to feel wiped out after sex?"

"You tell me. You're the one who figured it out." I'm lying flat on my stomach two feet away from him, not interested in moving a single goddamn muscle, and... is it just the two of us on the bed? Can't see any other bodies.

"Did not," he snarks. "I just remembered, is all."

"He says to the amnesic king of Neverland," I mutter. "Nothing more, nothing less. Damn, I should ask Wendy to magic me some smokes."

"Fuck that." He lifts a hand to jab a finger at me, then lets it drop by his head. "You remember now, too."

It's not an actual question so I just lift my head and peer at him. "That was a big thing for all of us to forget, and for so long."

"It was part of the deal," he says quietly, rolling his head toward me. "Part of the way this was supposed to work."

"That we slaver for the good of humanity without a clue as to the why?"

"Humans do it all the time," he says and I'm caught in his pretty green eyes.

"And we are gods in human bodies," I whisper. "How poetic."

"You mean inconvenient?"

"No. I like it." I make a show of looking him up and down. "My human body likes your human body."

Tink grins, coppery lashes shadowing his gaze. "Your dick sure does."

"My dick and I are in agreement," I state.

"I bet you are."

I grin back at him. "Your cock seems interested, too."

"I don't talk to my dick."

"Maybe you should," I tell him. "Mine has a lot to say."

"You're weird."

"And that's a shocker to you, how?"

Tink finally relaxes. Wound up tighter than a clock spring, this guy. And I've always wanted to take away the fear from his eyes, the tension from his strong body and replace it with something else.

Something more pleasurable.

"Where is Wendy?" I ask, reaching out to touch his hair. Such outrageous colors. So beautiful.

"The others are bathing her. Making sure she's okay after our orgy."

"Good." I glance at the door. Tink does, too. We both would like to be there with her, bather her and take care of her. Aftercare. But not yet. "Come here, Tink."

"What?"

"Just... come here."

He comes reluctantly, a suspicious glint in his green eyes. "Why?"

"Can I touch you?"

He swallows hard, his Adam's apple bobbing in his throat. "What if I touched you instead?"

Well, that's what I call fucking progress, but I just smirk. "Go ahead. Don't worry, I won't fuck you. Not unless you ask nicely."

"Asshole."

"I just want to hold you, fucker." I open my arms. "Let me?"

He produces a small uncertain sound that goes straight to my heart and—I won't deny it—to my dick. But I meant what I said. And I can hardly believe it when he scoots closer and with one last dubious glance at my face, he presses himself to me, slinging an arm over my hip.

It's... fucking nice. I gather him close, burying my nose in his fresh-smelling hair and sigh in contentment. "You've never let me do this before."

"Damn right I haven't," he says, muffled against my shoulder.

"What made you change your mind?"

He snickers softly. "You mean apart from the whole end-of-the-world situation?"

"Yeah. You slept with Wendy and now you let me hold you. That's more than you've allowed in centuries."

A small shrug of broad shoulders. "I wouldn't call getting over trauma changing my mind."

"Right." I huff. "You know what I mean."

"Well, I'm a god now. Can't let fear govern me."

"Too incendiary?" I suggest.

"Too stupid. Too cowardly."

"You've never been stupid," I inform him. "Or cowardly."

A bright flush spreads on his cheekbones. He rolls his eyes to give me a narrow look. "Goddammit, you really mean that."

"And don't ever fucking doubt it." I snort, making light of it. He actually thought I considered him stupid and a coward when I've loved him all this time for being the bright spark he is? "Fucking god of light. *You*. I mean, come on."

"Hey, I'm all rainbows and prancing unicorns, I'll have you know."

I kiss his brow. "I bet you are. In your dreams."

"I could smite you where you stand. Well," he amends, "where you lie."

"That would be inconvenient," I tell him. "You'd never get the stains out of the sheets."

He laughs, closes his eyes. Unable to resist, I kiss his brow and he sighs. It sounds like pleasure.

"Tink..."

"It will all be over soon, right?" he whispers. "She will remember and admit to her final fear and even this small piece of solid ground, this bit of paradise will crumble and we will go down with it. We may be gods but we're inhabiting human bodies. Well, human and Fae. No mermaids to save us now for their own nefarious ends."

I nuzzle his hair. "What will we do without the mermaids, huh? Reminds me of a poem..."

"Fuck your poems." He turns a little in my arms, runs a hand over my side. "You said I can touch."

"Uh, sure." His touch is electrifying. A shudder goes though me. "Be my guest."

It feels forbidden—because he's never willingly touched me before and I stopped trying to get through his defenses long ago. I mean, I spent whole centuries half out of my mind, so that wasn't all that difficult, in retrospect.

There was a lingering ache, though, in my mind, where I kept hoping he'd trust me enough to let me in.

But maybe it wasn't a matter of trusting me, but of trusting himself, of dealing with his own traumas, traumas we never discussed.

"You never asked me outright," Tink says, as if reading my mind. "Why I've been the way I am."

"Sarcastic as fuck?"

"Not wanting anyone to touch me."

"I could guess well enough." I lean back to get a look at his face. "Do you want to talk about it now?"

"Not now," he says quietly, his hand smoothing down my thigh, then circling down, between my legs. "There are better things to do. Don't you think?"

"Fuck, yeah." I groan when he wraps his hand around my cock. I'm hardening so fast I'm dizzy. "Tink... damn, you don't have to—"

"Shut up," he growls and scoots down my body, pushing my right knee up and putting his mouth on my cock.

Is it a diversion from the actual sex act, a way to cope with the fear, or does he really like giving head? I don't know and I don't ask. I said I won't force him to do anything he doesn't want, but if he's willing to go this far, who am I to argue?

Especially since... *ah fuck...* he gives really good head, sucking hard on my dick, his tongue playing on the underside, his hand fondling my balls, taking me from hard to holy-shit-I'm-gonna-blow-my-load-right-the-fuck-now in a blink.

How long have I craved this?

Almost as long as I've hoped for Jas to return to us.

Almost as long as I've hoped for the right girl to find me, find us, save us in every way—accept us. Want us as we are. Despite of what we are.

For what we are.

Tink knows exactly what we are, knew it before I ever did, recalled things I had lost and here he is—sucking me deep, and *oh fuck...* I can't fucking help the rocking of my hips, can't help thrusting into his mouth.

Roughly and expertly, too expertly for someone who hasn't allowed me to touch him, who hasn't allowed any sexual touch in centuries has any right to be—and I try not to think why, how he knows so much, what his mouth was used for before he came to me, not now—he coaxes me right to the brink and lets me hover there, cursing and shivering and grabbing for his head, his silky hair twining around my fingers, snagging them in knots—

"Fuck!" I tumble and crash into pleasure and relief and he swallows it all, sucking and forcing more pleasure into me until I can't fucking take anymore and shove him away. "Fuck..."

He hums something that might be a reply and draws back, looking up at me from beneath lowered lashes. "Good, huh?"

"Dammit, Tink, come up here."

He comes willingly once more and I can't believe my luck, that not only do I have Jas and Wendy back with us but also him. "What?"

"I need you," I growl. "Your turn."

"Uh-uh." He shakes his head, though his eyes sparkle. "We're going to bathe Wendy now."

"We are?" I'm confused. I thought we were getting somewhere.

"Yeah."

"But, Tink—"

He's already getting up, running a hand through his hair. It's mostly pink and copper, no signs of distress, though the look in his eyes is dark and thoughtful. "Come on."

Still addled by pleasure, I follow suit, swinging my legs off the bed, getting up. The signs slowly filter in.

He's not ready.

He's making progress, but I shouldn't push. The step he has taken is a giant one for him and I may not recall much from the past, before and after the island, but I know he's forcing himself to move forward and that's not something you rush.

"Yeah," I say, slant him a quick smile. "You're right. Let's go see how our Lady is doing."

The only one for us. The only one who could take in all this darkness and make it hers. In mortal or immortal form, she had always been our salvation.

21

WENDY

When the guys suggested I should take a bath to ease the aches from last night's activities, I didn't know what to expect.

Except for a bathtub, of course.

So I decided that this house has one, outside, a sunken pool at the edge of the terrace overlooking the sea—can't say I find the sea relaxing all of a sudden, but with the trees growing on either side, it has a secluded feeling—and that's where I find myself now, relaxing in the warm water.

With my guys around me.

Well, we left Peter and Tink still asleep in the bedroom, but Jas and the Twins are right there, in the water with me, soaping me up and running their hands all over me.

It feels good. My ass is sore. I hadn't felt the pain much last night. My pussy is a little tender, my nipples hurt as if someone has bitten them—which I'm pretty sure happened—and other parts of me feel chafed and abused.

But I don't mind. On the contrary, I like it, I like the proof of last night, because last night was glorious and I want more of it, more of them. I hope it was a prelude to much more to come.

A prelude to the future, perhaps?

I don't know why I'm scared to think of the future. Maybe it's what Tink implied, that it will all end soon.

But I can't think of that now.

Not when Wes pulls me to sit on his lap, his hands roaming over my breasts. I hiss as my achy ass rubs against his hard-on, but he only rubs and lightly pinches my nipples, making me shiver and arch a little against him. My head falls back on his muscular shoulder as he caresses me, kissing my neck.

Jas and Colt, meanwhile, have set to cleaning each other, soaping each other's bodies and kissing, which is... my God, it's so sexy and distracting. From heavy-lidded eyes I watch as they soap up each other's asses, pressing their bodies together, and then lean back to soap each other's hard cocks.

So hot.

So frigging hot I barely notice when Wes' hands trail down my belly to touch me between my legs. I gasp when he circles my clit with his finger, then rubs with his other hand right where I ache and plunges two fingers inside me.

Aching and yet primed, I orgasm right then and there, rocking on his fingers, moaning.

"You're so sexy," Wes breathes in my ear and I moan again, waves of pleasure buffeting me. Slowly he slips his fingers out of me and even that feels so good. "I want you."

Jas and Colt are now both turned toward us, eyes dark, hands on their cocks, stroking, and the sight of that makes me choke on another moan, my pussy clenching.

It's like a call for them.

They fall on me like ravenous wolves, pressing themselves to me, kissing and touching every part of my body they can reach.

Colt lifts my legs and buries his face between them, licking and sucking, while Jas fucks my mouth with his tongue, and another orgasm is building inside of me.

Wes' rock-hard cock slides up and down the small of my back, pressing between my ass cheeks, and he groans in my ear. It burns where he's rubbing from last night's action, but the pain feeds into the loop of pleasure.

Colt's tongue lashes against my clit, then stabs into my pussy, and I come undone again, crying out against Jas's lips, thrashing in the water.

When I can see and hear and breathe again, I'm floating in the warm water in Wes' arms, gazing blearily up at the sunny sky, my body lax and strangely loose and disjointed, like my thoughts.

Thoughts about the sea and the mermaids.

About my family and the past.

About gods and goddesses, reincarnations and manifestations, dreams and reality.

Just then, someone clears his throat.

"Well, I never. You started without us? I thought you were just going to soap her up and let her soak to ease the aches from last night," Peter says and I crane my head to see him standing at the main house door.

Standing beside him, Tink chuckles, low and throaty and dark, reaching down to stroke his hardening cock.

They head toward us and I narrow my eyes at them. Something has changed between them, I can feel it from here, something in their bond has shifted and relaxed while binding them more tightly together.

Peter slings his arm over Tink's shoulders as they reach the pool, hauling Tink to his side, and Tink allows it, a small smirk on his face.

Both of them are as naked as the day they were born—like all of us—their powerful bodies magnificently muscled, their handsome faces drawn in pleased lines, their big cocks hardening and rising against their taut stomachs as they gaze at us.

"Of course we started without you, lazy assholes," Colt growls, sitting back on his heels in the water. "Fucking sleepyheads. You barely twitched when we got up earlier."

"Hm. So let's make up for lost time," Peter says, pulling Tink along and jumping into the pool.

They both splash into the water and resurface seconds later, shaking their shaggy heads like dogs—and why does my heart lose a beat?

Water will never be my element.

Some traumas are rooted too deep, even for a goddess.

"Time is never lost," I whisper as they both wade toward us. "You slept together."

Colt and Jas exchange looks.

"Is she saying what I think she's saying?" Wes breathes at my back. "Tink, you guys fucked?"

"Yeah, we fucked," Tink says, though there's a flat note in his voice now. "Move aside."

Peter glances at him, gives a little shake of his head I can't interpret, then takes me out of Wes' arms and into his own, to straddle his thighs. "Where were we?"

"You weren't," Colt says, giving him a shove in the ribs. "We were. You literally jumped in just now."

Peter grabs him around the neck, pulls him in for a kiss all lips and teeth and tongue that has Colt groaning and gripping Peter's shoulder.

Then Peter breaks the kiss and turns back to me, slightly out of breath. He licks his lips. "My turn."

"For what?" I whisper.

"To fuck you," he says and grabs my legs, settles them around his hips, and is already pushing into me.

God... I pant as he drives his cock deep in one long thrust— then groan when Wes presses his body to mine from behind, bending me forward, opening me up more only to position his cock against Peter's and push inside my pussy, too.

Twofer.

Jesus.

I gasp, unable to draw breath, drowning as he slowly slips into me, spreading me so wide it burns and hurts, and though I whimper, I don't want them to stop. I'm slippery enough inside that it makes the passage easier but holy shit, it's so tight. Their cocks are so big I sometimes wonder how one of them fits in there, let alone two.

Still can't believe I had two up my ass last night—and now...

Peter puts his mouth to my neck and bites down.

"Please..." I whisper. "Harder. Draw blood."

"I haven't even kissed you yet," he breathes.

"This is better than kissing," I tell him. "This is who you are."

He growls like a wild animal, his eyes turning into dark pools of need. His hands on my hips are bruising, grinding my bones. Wes' hands are on my waist, so I take them and lift them to my breasts until he grabs them and squeezes.

"Yes," I moan, "yes..."

A creature made for pain and pleasure, that's who I am. I accept it now, I know it. Since the dawn of time, I have been torn between light and dark, life and death, delight and agony, and these men are my companions, my husbands, each one suited to a manifestation of me.

But above all, they are all suited to Wendy Darling, the woman I am.

They fit my *soul.*

As they both thrust into me, the others gather round, Colt fisting my hair, tugging, Jas gripping my arm and thrusting his cock against my side, growling, while Tink trails his fingers over my mouth, dipping two inside, forcing me to suck on them as if it were his cock.

They are all a part of me. I need them. I love them in a way

I've never loved before. I desire them and feel for them and miss them. Need them to touch me, grip me, mark me.

Never thought I'd feel this way for a man, let alone so many —and it makes this rock of an island feel like home in a way that my family home and the apartment I share with Charlie never has.

And the pressure is mounting, reaching critical mass as they fuck me and touch me and hurt me and pleasure me. My core clenches, spasms, and with a wail, I let go.

I come and it's so intense I almost black out, dark crowding my vision, making my head too light, my body too heavy. My entire body pulses and throbs, clenches and releases, again and again. My men lean in closer, bowing over me, the cocks inside me jerking and shooting wet heat.

I'm burning from the inside out, a star gone supernova.

Dying and being born again.

Bursting with life as I court death.

Loving what I should hate but…

I shudder and strong arms come around me, enclosing me in a circle of warm bodies in the cooling water.

"What's wrong?" Peter asks softly.

"I liked it," I breathe, my voice hitching. "I liked it way too much. The violence. The pain."

"But that's great. Perfect, really. What's the problem?"

I rest my forehead against Peter's shoulder. "Is this a godly thing? To like the things you shouldn't? To like what is wrong for you?"

"What the fuck are you talking about? What is wrong with liking this?"

"Nothing… nothing is wrong with *this*." I'm panting, unable to catch my breath. "I'm talking about the past."

"What about the past?" Jas says, his hand gentling on my hair, stroking instead of pulling. "What's this about?"

"My father..." I swallow hard, leaning back against Wes, their gazes on me as I half-float in the water. "I..."

I gasp when Wes and then Peter pull out of me. I'm sore but I'm kind of lost inside my mind right now, the pain distant.

"What about that asshole?" Tink says, voice quiet but lethal, his fingers caressing my face. "What else has he done to you?"

"Nothing. It's me. All me. I know what is my final fear," I whisper. "You have to know, I have many fears. Fear of rejection, fear of change, fear of thunderstorms, and let us not forget my famous fear of the sea. But there is one fear that governs me, a fear that is part shame and regret, part anger and frustration. A fear from my past."

"And what is it?" Jas asks.

I draw a deep breath, but it doesn't help my reedy voice. "I... I enjoyed my dad's attention." I have to draw another breath, choking, suffocating on air. "The fact he found me pretty, prettier than Mom. That he focused on me, bought me little gifts, dresses and shoes. It made me feel... good."

"Nothing wrong with that," Colt says gently. "Wendy... What else did he do to you?"

I shake my head, shuddering. "Nothing. He never... you know." I swallow hard.

"It wasn't your fault, girl."

"You don't understand." I shake my head. "Mom knew all about this, and she was jealous, and I shouldn't have liked any of it, shouldn't have accepted the attention, but... Mom never paid me any. Never wanted me around—but Dad did, and I liked it too damn much. It's my fault, all that happened afterward. All that happened to me, I deserved it."

"Wendy," Peter says, "*no.*"

"I deserved to drown and die." I close my eyes. "That's what I'm afraid of. That I deserved it and cheated fate somehow."

"But it wasn't your fault, Wendy," Tink whispers, his green

eyes wide. "What your father did isn't on you. You were a child. It's not on you at all. Wendy... Do you see it now?"

"I think..." I try again. "Yes. I know now that what he did wasn't okay. Even if I liked his attention."

"It doesn't matter," Jas says.

"What the fuck, man?" Colt hisses. "Shut your mouth."

"It doesn't matter," Jas says again, "because this isn't about whether she was guilty or not. And for the record, she definitely wasn't guilty of anything. But it's about a fear she had to face."

We all consider his words for a long moment.

"And have you?" Peter asks eventually, gazing at me. "Have you faced that fear now, Wendy?"

"Accept who you are," I whisper to myself. "Accept the past. Is that what you're asking? If I've I faced my fear? If I can let it go?"

"Yeah, that's the question, isn't it?" Tink murmurs.

I dig through the memories, the feelings. "I carried this weight of guilt for all this time, but I was just a kid. He abused me. Both of my parents did. But what they did doesn't define me, and didn't change me. I am who I am, I like what I like. And if I like pain mixed with my pleasure, well, that's my prerogative and it has nothing to do with my past and everything to do with my preferences. I choose rough sex. I like it. It's my thing, and it's nobody else's business."

"Damn right it's nobody else's business," Wes says. "You and us, we like it that way and it's nobody's business but ours."

"Yes, that, exactly." A weight has lifted off my chest, off my mind. Smiling, I open my eyes, open my mouth to thank them, to tell them I love them, that I'm right where I want to be—

A deafening crash shakes us. The ground trembles and heaves, throwing us all into the water of the pool. Spluttering, Wes tries to sit back up, hauling me up with him, but the ground shakes again and a splintering crack rends the air.

The island is sinking. The last part of it, the last part standing.

The last fear gone.

"Watch out!" I shout, grabbing at them, gathering them close to me, making sure I'm touching them all because somehow, I feel it's important, so important, quintessential that I touch them as we go down. "Hold onto me!"

And then we fall through water and air and rock and darkness.

The bridge is no more.

22

WENDY

Expecting the buffeting of the elements, I raise my arms the moment I open my eyes to protect myself—but there's nothing.

Quiet.

I'm lying someplace dim, soft and warm. Where is the water, the rocks, the dark wind blowing us away like leaves?

Is this death? Is it the afterlife?

Lowering my arms, I pat my face, my chest. I seem to be whole and alive. My heart is beating, my lungs are filling with sweet oxygen—and this place smells and feels familiar.

In fact, I know the shape of that window, the shadow of the old chair heaped high with clothes, the white vanity and the old Pink Floyd poster on the wall.

My room. I'm back in the apartment and...

Wait.

I sit up and something small and hard rolls and pings over my arm. I grab for it. A small, golden acorn—and a gasp escapes me as my memory becomes *peopled*.

I wasn't alone when that gale hit—no, not a gale but when the *island collapsed*. I was with *people*, I was with my guys.

Where are my men? Where are the Lost Boys?

I turn and hit something, something warm and solid, and I yelp, my heart slamming against my ribs. What is—?

"Where the *fuck*," a male voice says by my ear, scaring the bejesus out of me, "are we?"

———

"You're here!" I throw my arms around as many of the boys as I can reach—Peter, and Tink, and Colt... "Where's Wes? And Jas?"

"Present and accounted for," Jas says, getting up from the floor, rubbing at the back of his head. "The landing wasn't perfect, I must say, girl. You need to work on that."

"Yeah, you could work a little on the dynamics of inter-dimensional traveling," Wes drawls, taking Jas' proffered hand and getting to his feet with a wince. "Oof."

I laugh breathlessly, my eyes swimming with tears, going through emotions so fast I can't quite grasp them—confusion, panic, shock, fear, joy.

So much joy.

"You didn't die." I bury my face in Colt's shoulder because he's the nearest to me. "We didn't die. We didn't sink with the island."

"No, you brought us here," he says quietly. "With you."

"Holy fuck," Tink says, blinking wide eyes. "We're in the human world?"

"Looks like it," Peter says. "We're in your apartment, aren't we?"

"Yeah," I whisper. "You are."

"Hell." Wes takes a few steps, stops at the window. "Never thought I'd ever come back to this world."

"None of us did," Colt says. "We were meant to go down with the island."

"Or so you assumed," I say, curling my arm around Peter's neck. I'm grinning so widely my cheeks hurt. "As it turns out, not everything was supposed to go as you thought, was it?"

"No," Peter says softly, "it wasn't."

"You accomplished your mission. The bridge between the worlds is all gone."

"It is," he says, his voice kind of breathless.

"Was that really what we had to do?"

He shakes his head, his shaggy dark hair falling into his eyes. "I thought it was. But maybe a bridge is necessary."

"Maybe it has always been there." I consider the possibility. "A soul bridge. A dream bridge."

"Maybe." He smiles down at me. "You will rebuild it, over time."

"That's what you expect?"

"That's what you do," he tells me, intense and sweet like honey. "It's who you are. You will rebuild it with dreams instead of nightmares. You will make the island rise and bloom, with its benevolent little mermaids and red birds or crabs instead of murderous machines. You will fix it. You have done so in the past."

"Persephone has, you mean," I mutter.

"And that is who you are."

"Still?" I ask. "You think so? Now that the mission is over?"

"But you have to rebuild…" Peter trails off. "Holy shit, could it be true?"

"What do you mean?" Jas says.

"Maybe we're not gods anymore," Tink whispers, "only men. Our mission has been accomplished. We can be released from our promise."

"No more gods and men in one body," Peter mutters. "No more divinity, no more magic and miracles. Just mortals."

"That," I say firmly, "is good enough for me."

He gives me a startled look. "But without being Persephone... you'd still want us? Be with us?"

"It's not Persephone who wanted you," I inform him. "Not Persephone who loves you. It's me."

"But—"

"She was in me, but she wasn't me." I wink at him. "I, Wendy Darling, love all five of you."

"But do you expect us... to change?" Jas says, flexing his hands. He seems to be doing it unconsciously, a frown on his face. "Be nice and gentle, be normal, fit right into society?"

"What about our shadows?" Peter whispers. "I don't think we got rid of them. Not sure we can."

And that's a big clue but I don't mention it, because I don't know what it means that they still have shadows, still have souls. I don't know what we are anymore, either.

One thing is for sure:

"I don't want you to change," I say.

"We will *try* to fit in," Colt says, cuffing Peter on the back of the head. "You're not a king anymore, got it? We'll need to work, make ends meet, like everyone else."

"You'll always be our king," Tink says, "don't listen to Colt. But he's right that we have to try, Peter. No more fighting, no more battles. No war. Just life."

"It won't be easy," Peter says. "Remember the shadow problem."

"Not a problem," I tell him and meet his blue gaze square on. "That's how you were when I met you and I never wanted to save you from yourselves. Only from the other monsters. You are kind. You are decent people. After all, you put the fate of the worlds before your own lives and your own happiness."

"We will be okay," Wes whispers. "No more danger. No more madness. No more Reds and mermaids to fight. No more hating and fighting each other."

"No more looking for Wendy and the cure to the blight of the worlds," Colt says.

"But sex…" Peter leans in, bites lightly at my neck. "That can still be crazy and bloody."

"It had better be," I breathe. "I want—"

"Oh, God!" a woman's voice says from the door that is now standing ajar, and I see Charlie, a hand over her mouth, her eyes wide. "Okay, Wendy, who are all these hunks and why am I not invited to the party?"

————

"So let me get this straight. You found all these hot guys on an island that sank and brought them home with you?" Charlie asks.

"We lost everything," Peter says, dark brows knitted, tapping his fingers on the kitchen table around which we have all gathered. It's a tight fit with five broad-shouldered guys, Charlie and myself. "Wendy is helping us get back on our feet."

"She is, huh?" Charlie shoots me a narrow look. "What island was that? I don't recall reading about any island sinking on the news."

"A very small island," Tink says. "It would have never made the news."

"But it was our home," Wes gives Charlie a blinding smile that nevertheless manages to convey sadness. "Everything we owned was there."

"And now it's all under the waves," Colt adds.

Charlie turns her gaze on Jas who has been quiet since we sat down together. "That's a sad story."

"At least we are alive," Jas says gravely and Charlie shivers.

"We are alive and here, with Wendy," Wes says. "It's all we need."

"And we will start anew," Colt says.

"Is it okay if we stay here for now?" I ask her.

"*We*?" Her gaze returns to me. "Are you *leaving*?"

"It's five men and me. We can hardly all stay here in my room."

"You're going to…" She waves a hand between me and Jas, then the other guys. "Be with all of them?"

"Well… yeah." I can't help it; I grin and glance sideways at Tink who puts his hand over mine on the table. "That's the plan."

"Indeed, it is." Tink grins back.

Charlie mutters something that sounds like *"greedy biatch."*

"We have been lucky," Colt says. "Finding the right girl for us."

"If she'll still have us," Jas mutters.

"Will you still have us?" Peter asks.

"Always," I whisper, warmth seeping into my face. "Sorry, Charlie. I should have told you about this but…"

"But it's complicated?" She frowns.

"Yeah," Peter says, "because up until today we didn't know if we would live to be here."

"You knew the island might sink?" She blinks at him. She has a dazed look on her face.

"There were warning signs," he says darkly.

"Charlie." I turn to her. "Aren't you happy for me?"

"Happy? Damn, girl." She sighs, tearing her gaze off my men to look at me. "Of course I am happy for you, but couldn't you at least have brought back one hunk for me? That's not too much to ask, is it? It's what any good friend would have done. Honestly…"

23

PETER

"So..." Wes says, throwing himself down on the bed. "No more gods. Just us?"

"We think so," Colt mutters. "Doesn't change much, does it? We weren't even aware of it for the longest time."

I glance down at my hands. They're shaking. A junkie, a lost god, a king without a crown, now a mortal man.

I clench my hands, curl them int fists just as a smile curls my mouth. This world doesn't hurt anymore, but I'm still myself, with my flaws and my past. Not erased.

It's something to hold onto. I will fight the addiction.

My need for this group of people is much stronger.

"And what now?" Wes glances around at us. "Seriously, you guys. All our lives we've been fighting the Reds and the mermaids, looking for the right Wendy, battling to kill the nightmares. What are we gonna do here?"

"You're asking if we can live in peace," I say. "Without violence—well, outside of the bedroom. Without a goal."

"We have a goal," Tink says. "Our goal is to have a life with Wendy. To be happy."

"And how do you become happy?" Jas growls. "Tell us."

"Like this," Wendy says, approaching Jas from behind and wrapping her arms around him, resting her cheek against his back. "No?"

A smile flickers on Jas' face. "Perhaps," he concedes. "I'm not used to this. Not used to thinking like this. To having someone... Anyone."

He's staring down at his hand, and he's holding his crocodile skin watch. The glass is cracked and the hands are still. It has stopped. It really is over.

"You can get used to happiness," I tell him, coming to stand in front of him, settling a hand on his shoulder. "To being with people who care for you, fucker."

The watch clatters to the floor as Jas grabs me. "Show me," he rumbles and shoves my shirt up. "Where is it?"

Anyone else would demand to know what he means, but I know. Oh, I know.

"My scar? Here." I yank my shirt off and let it drop to the floor, then reach for Jas's. I haul it off his torso and I step closer. Reach out to touch the scar I put on him.

He does the same, a crease between his brows.

Damn.

Wendy steps around Jas to place a hand on his arm. Tink approaches from the other side, and the Twins are only a step behind. What brought us all together? Jas and me, we're mirror images of each other with our similar built, the matching scars, just as the Twins are, just as Tink is with Wendy.

Patterns. Patterns in the universe, which makes sense where gods are concerned. They just love symbols, repeating shapes and numbers, imposing an order on a chaotic world.

But the affection, the lust, the need... that's all us. We happened to find in each other what we need.

And now we finally have the time to explore those feelings and everything that surrounds them—the touches, the conversations, the understanding that will bind us even closer.

I tap lightly Jas's scar and lift my hand to pat his cheek and grip his jaw. "You with me, fucker? With us? Are you ready for the greatest adventure of your life? Even the gods don't get to experience this."

He frowns at me. "This?"

"Yeah, this. Having a family." I nod at Wendy. "Maybe some babies. A house. A garden. A car. Going to the movies—"

"Oh, yeah," Tink breathes.

"—and spending our nights and long weekends in bed, getting to know each other's bodies, each other's kinks and desires. Doesn't it sound fucking lovely?"

In reply, Jas grabs my arms, hauls me closer and kisses me. He tastes like sex and male and despair. I had expected Jas to be the best-suited of us to this life, the most convinced we can do it. After all, he spent his life trying to save us.

Perhaps he didn't think about saving himself in the process.

I'll take care of that. Of him. It's only fair. In love and war, all is fair, right? And I love him. I'm pretty damn sure all of us here do.

But the Twins close in on him, putting their arms around him, and Wendy slips between us to kiss him in her turn, and it makes me grin because he's kind of floundering, unsure what to do with all the attention.

It's goddamn sweet.

I catch Tink's eye and something shifts behind the green gaze. I'm not sure what it is, but it intrigues me and I move toward him.

He doesn't move away, watching me as I slide an arm around him. His eyes shift from me to Wendy who's now surrounded by the Twins and Jas. Jas is kissing her mouth, while Colt and Wes are kissing his jaw, his neck, gripping his hair and tugging.

Finally, Colt grabs Wendy, spins her toward him and kisses

her hard, Jas and Wes taking it up from there, kissing each other.

"All paired up," Tink breathes.

"Are we?" I wink at him and he heaves a breathless laugh.

"I guess we are," he says.

A few feet away, the knot of bodies untangles a little and Colt grabs Wendy around the waist, a feral snarl on his face. "Mine," he growls, dragging her to the bed.

"I think it's my turn," I say, winking at Tink.

"Bullshit," Colt says over his shoulder. "You had your turn with Wendy last time."

"With Tink," I continue, not taking my eyes off Tink. "My turn with Tink."

That has an interesting effect. All of them are now staring at us, questions in their eyes.

Tink's face reddens. He lifts his chin and pulls me to him, latching his mouth on mine. The kiss is hard, aggressive, punishing.

I fucking love it.

Don't get me wrong. I love Wendy's softness, I love how she yields to us, to our dark violence. But I also like guys, and this guy... well, I have a particularly soft spot for him.

He's hard, though, and that fucking pleases me. He's really into it, not just to give the others the finger. Over his shoulder, as we kiss, I see Colt on the bed with Wendy, her legs wrapped around his hips, I see Jas getting in behind her, Wes settling behind Colt. One big knot of sex and love.

I wish we could join them, and we will, later. Not necessarily today.

One thing at a time.

I have Tink to tame first, Tink to pleasure, to mark him so that he remembers it's good with me. That he has nothing to fear, that we won't do anything he doesn't want.

"Look at me," I say when he draws back, breathing hard,

eyes a little wild. My lips throb from his kiss. I think he bit me. It was fucking great. "It's me, fucker."

"I know it's you," he hisses, "think I'd be kissing you otherwise?" but his gaze latches on mine like a lifeline just as his hands grip my biceps, blunt nails digging into my flesh.

"Just don't fucking forget it," I growl as I grab him, as I turn him and shove him against a white vanity table with a round mirror Wendy has furnished her room with.

"Dammit, Peter," he snarls, shoving back, but his ass only finds my crotch and my painful hard-on.

He freezes.

"Want it or not?" I lean over him to breathe in his ear. "Are you ready for it or not yet? The truth, dammit."

"I am, yeah, give it to me. I have to... have to get over it." His breath hitches. "Do it."

"I'll make it good," I promise him.

"Whatever, I don't fucking care." He's already panting, half in arousal and half in fear, I'll bet. "I want it over with."

"Do you, fucker?" I yank his pants down and he hisses, bucking. He's so not ready, it makes me furious with him that he's pushing himself into this. "Just because Wendy felt ready to face her fears doesn't mean you have to rush yourself, you know."

"Shut up and fuck me already."

My dick should have some morals and say, *hey, the guy's not ready*, and deflate, but all his struggling and all the angst are making me harder than a stripper pole.

Let's be honest, I'm no saint. I like that he's still afraid, that he's still unsure, even if he wants it to happen.

I get the need to face the fear, to get it over with, ready or not, hoping for the best.

I grab for a cream I see on the table and coat my fingers in it, stroke between his taut ass cheeks and dip a finger into his asshole.

He tenses, curses. Tries to shove me back.

"Look." I grip his chin and lift it until he's looking at himself, at us, in the mirror. "Look at you, so fucking hot, so fucking pretty." He growls, shakes his head and I chuckle. "Don't like the word? So fucking handsome, then. Look at those eyes, that mouth, holy fuck... Look at that body. I've wanted you for so damn long."

He doesn't buck again, his eyes widening a little, and I don't know if it's from the way my finger is stroking him inside or from what I'm saying. It's not my usual style to offer compliments during sex, but damn, he's worth it.

"And look at them on the bed going at it," I go on, my own gaze flicking again to the mirror. "Watch as they fuck Wendy."

"Fucking hot," Tink whispers.

"Damn right."

But so is Tink, bent over, his muscular ass at my mercy, my finger stroking, probing, searching—until I find his prostate and he gasps and shudders.

I add a second finger, opening him up as we both watch Wendy getting nailed by the Twins in turn, while Jas takes her ass.

Tink groans something that might be a curse.

It's a good distraction, watching the others, drawing his attention away from what I'm doing to him. One day, when he's one hundred percent ready, a distraction won't be needed, but I'm so damn proud of him for working through his trauma.

And fuck, yeah, the distraction is damn arousing, and the need to be with Wendy is ever present, but we're still the individuals we once were. Despite the newness of the situation, of this relationship with her, we can still fuck and kiss and help and tease each other.

The reminder is also needed.

And I need him. He may not know it, not realize what he

means to me, what all this means and how much I love and desire all of them, and maybe it's time to talk.

So as I pull my fingers out and shove my cock into him, inch by inch, keeping a groan between my teeth, I tell him the truth.

"I fucking love you, Tinker. You know that, right? I've loved you from the start and that won't ever change. Get it?"

He gasps, moans, bucks, and I grab his hips to stop him from moving and clenching like that because I'm two milliseconds away from shooting my load. "Damn you."

"What?"

"You, asshole," he manages, "now you decide to tell me?"

I chuckle, then hiss when he clenches around my dick again. "It seemed like a good time. Do you—?"

"Holy fuck." He reaches between his legs and starts to jack off as I fuck him. "So good..."

Okay, good, we're on track here, and I brace one hand on the creaking vanity table so I can fuck him harder, faster. Feelings take the back seat as my body grabs the reins and we rut together, cursing and grunting. Small jars and bottles fall and crash to the floor. The table creaks ominously with our thrusts.

Then Wendy's voice rises in a wail as she comes, and the sound shoots straight to my balls.

Tink seems affected, too, because his hand is now moving frantically over his cock, his ass tightening around my dick. "Fuck. God. Oh, fuck."

I join in the litany, feeling my balls drawing up, my cock twitching and swelling more, feeling the tension coil at the base, ready to break.

Bending my head, I bite lightly at Tink's neck, then harder, leaving a love bite, a bruise, a hickey, and he jerks and cries out, his ass clamping down on my cock. His cum splashes on the table, and I shove my dick as deep as I can, my breath leaving me as I come, the pleasure as sharp as the relief of finally touching him.

"Fuck," he gasps, "I love you, too, goddammit. Fuck!"

I grin.

Panting, gasping, we hold onto the small table, riding the aftershocks, and I lick at the bruise I left on his neck. It makes me happy to see it there.

I hope he feels it for many days to come.

"You okay?" I finally manage.

"Better than ever," he says and all is good with the world.

24

JAS

Seeing Peter and Tink together is a sight I'll never forget. It stays with me long after we doze and wake up, shower and sit around the apartment, trying to wrap our heads around everything we know, everything we thought we knew and this new reality.

Peter thrusting into Tink, whispering in his ear, his dark hair a shadow against Tink's copper and pink locks.

I don't know if the hot feeling in my chest, in my head, if it's jealousy, anger, or pure dark desire.

Peter's taste lingers on my tongue. That kiss I stole from him earlier, it was everything and yet not enough. I've missed him for centuries, died over and over with my need for him, for everything about him, from his voice, to his eyes to the shape of him.

His warm, strong body pressed to mine.

Despite all he said, despite giving into my demanding mouth earlier, he probably doesn't want to be around me. He probably wants to punch my face.

Strange he hasn't done it yet.

How do I trust he has forgiven me? While I need to possess

him as he's possessed my thoughts all this time, obsessed me, held me prisoner without even realizing.

A willing captive.

I've fallen for all of them, watching them over time, especially lately, but it's him I want most of all.

He's the one I started out to save.

I lean back against the wall, folding my arms over my chest, I stay quiet as the bathroom door opens and Tink emerges, clad in a sheet wound around his waist, heading for the bedroom.

He crosses paths with Peter who reaches out to ruffle Tink's hair in passing, a smirk on his mouth.

Peter who is only clad in dark pants, his feet bare, shirtless with that scar I gave him calling to me.

I unfold my arms, watching as he enters the bathroom and closes the door.

I rub at my own scar through my shirt.

And opening the bathroom door, I follow him inside.

He's inside the shower stall, water running. The thought of him naked makes my fucking heart race.

Peter, I say, just his name, my hands clenching at my sides.

I need to face him, confront him, I need to touch him, I need... him. This collision between us has long been in the cards.

Shedding my shirt, losing my pants, I pad through the small bathroom. Through the rising vapor, through the misted glass, I see his powerful form.

I open the door and he whirls about, a frown on his face.

Jas. His voice is quiet—not harsh, not angry. His eyes glance over my body, darkening, then return to my face. Want to join me?

I lift my hand, slide it over one powerful shoulder, gripping it. The scar is mocking me, stark against his skin. "Fisher King," I whisper.

"Don't," he says, then he puts his hands on my hips and

hauls me inside. "That name doesn't fit anymore. The wound has healed."

"Has it?" My own scar aches as the warm water beats down on us, as I drown in his eyes. "How the fuck do you expect me to believe it?"

"Jas..." His hands slide up my chest, cup my face. "Look at me. Look at us. We won this battle. And we found each other again. I found you."

"How can you trust me?" I ask bitterly. "After so long?"

"Because I want to trust you. I want you back. You were my first."

"Your first nightmare?"

"My first love. My first ray of light. I can't fucking believe..." His lashes lower. "Can't believe I can touch you again like this."

"You don't hate me?" I snarl a little, annoyed at letting slip the question. "Don't you—"

He grabs my face and kisses me, hard. My mind empties and I find myself leaning in, groaning at the sting of his teeth on my mouth, his tongue thrusting against mine, his muscular body molding to mine.

Yes, fuck, yes...

At least I can tell he wants me, I think fuzzily, as his cock stirs and stars hardening between us. His kiss spears through me, a punch of desire going straight to my balls. I kiss him back with all I have, all the fucking despair and fucking misery that's seeped into me through time, when I thought I'd never have this again, never have him.

He bites my lip.

I bite back. Then I push him back against the tiled wall and it's all teeth and tongues and lips and stubble, our bodies rubbing together, cocks dueling.

When we break apart for a snatch of air, he arches his neck and after all of a moment's hesitation, I worry his skin with my teeth, leaving a hickey.

He doesn't stop me.

I'm breathing hard, hope warring with wariness. I brush his cheek, lick his chin, pinch his nipple, grab his hair and pull his head further back.

He's not wearing his golden acorn and I'm not wearing my crocodile watch. No more magic, no more masks. We're both laid bare, and I don't know what the fuck to do with him, how to do all the things I want to him.

Punish him for making me feel so much.

Punish myself for staying away for so long.

Worshipping him as he deserves. Taking him so brutally he'll feel it forever.

"I watched you," I murmur and he gazes at me from under his dark lashes, his back arching as I keep pulling on his hair. "I watched and wished…"

"I did hate you," he says and takes advantage of my flinch to grab my neck and bring our foreheads together. "Because I wasn't allowed to be with you anymore. Because I had to accept that you didn't want me anymore, that you wanted me dead."

"Never. Fuck, never."

"I know that now. Wish you'd told me. Wish you'd come clean."

"There's nothing clean," I growl, "about all I'd do for you, Peter, all I want to do to you."

"Good," he says. "There's nothing clean about me, either. I'm filthy to the dregs of my black soul."

"You're fucking beautiful," I inform him and push away from him only to turn him around. In the confines of the shower stall it isn't easy and he growls at me, but goes willingly, placing his hands on the tiled wall. When I press my chest to his broad back, my cock to his muscular ass, he shudders. "And damn hot."

"Will you fuck me, then," he murmurs, "or not?"

"Fuck." I tangle my fingers in his wet hair again, grip his

hip, needing to hold onto him. "Do you remember when we last did this?"

"It's been way too long."

Every point where our bodies touch, I ache. I run my nose over his neck, inhaling his scent. "I almost killed you once."

"You're killing me now, Jas."

"Don't joke about it."

"Jas..." He lets out a breath. "How can I get it through that thick remorseful skull of yours? We both did things we regret. But I don't hate you, Jas. I fucking love you, you idiot."

A slow explosion inside my head. His words are fireworks, burning the back of my eyes, scrambling my thoughts.

"And I've been waiting for you to come to me."

"You were? But you were with Tink."

"I love him, too. I love all of you. But this, right now, is about us. About reforging what we broke."

Yeah, this is about us. In the warm mist of the shower, with our bodies pressed together, there's only us, our painful past and the blinding brilliance of the future.

"Don't fucking make me wait any longer," he growls. "I've waited enough centuries. Here." He grabs something from the shower shelf—a small bottle and I squint at it. "Use this."

"Conditioner?"

"It's a cream. It will do."

I squeeze out a generous dollop—it smells like coconut, I think—and shove the bottle blindly back on the shelf. Smearing the cream between Peter's ass cheeks feels like a ritual, like a sacred act. My fingers remember how to do this even if my mind has tried to bury the memories—they hurt too fucking bad.

I push my fingers into him, slowly opening him up, stroking him inside until his breathing becomes harsh and he starts rocking back.

He folds one arm on the wall and rests his forehead on it. "Fuck, Jas…"

"Haven't had a man do you in a while?"

"Not since you," he says quietly and my mind is blown at the admission. My cock jumps, heavy and aching.

His ass swallows my fingers, clenching, making me moan.

"You're my undoing," he whispers and I kiss the back of his neck, so vulnerable and pale, his dark hair curling, the wings of his shoulder blades jutting out sharply. His broad ribcage cuts in sharply at his waist and narrow hips, and his ass is sculpted from marble. "Get on with it."

I almost laugh at his impatience. I never thought I'd be allowed this pleasure, this happiness again, and if I did, I'd take all the time in the world to prepare him, but it feels good to know I'm not the only one desperate.

That I wasn't the only one who missed him.

There's enough cream left on my hand to lather my stiff cock with, and then I position myself at his entrance and push.

He resists me, and I bite lightly at his neck, rub at his hip, demanding entrance.

I don't expect to be swallowed in so suddenly, and a cry escapes me, despite my best efforts. Hadn't intended to bare myself to the bone, allow myself to fall to fucking pieces just by sinking into him, but good lord, I am. I'm falling apart.

And his submission is so sweet it shatters me even more. It destroys me.

He groans, trembles, head bowed, and I resist the urge to start thrusting. He doesn't give me an option, though, thrusting back, fucking himself on my cock.

"Peter, dammit…" Coherent thought unravels. Slamming my hand on the wall by his head, I start fucking him in earnest, pounding his ass, lost in his body, in his raw beauty, in the connection we once shared and now share again.

Still can't believe he lets me.

Still can't believe he initiated the kiss this time, that he turned willingly, letting me top him.

Can't believe I deserve a second chance, because I did all I did to save him, save them all, and still I felt like the thug of the story.

Maybe because everyone thought the same for so long, it's ingrained, engraved in my bones.

It doesn't matter.

As long as he'll have me.

As long as he'll forgive me.

Fuck... oh fuck. I thrust into his tight ass again and again, my thoughts cracking and breaking, crumbling to dust. My past starts to crumble as I fuck him, the water raining on us, warm and clean as I screw him in the filthiest way possible.

"Peter," I groan. I'm going to come, going to explode, going to die in this perfect moment. "I can't fucking lose you again."

"You won't," Peter breathes, reaching with one hand behind to grip my forearm, hard enough to cut off circulation. "Never... never, do you hear me? Never again."

"I only wanted to save you."

"And you did. Only you," he says, his voice punctuated by my thrusts, "fuck, you're the only one stronger than me, the one who can take care of me. I need you, Jas."

"Holy fuck..." I bite at his neck, his shoulder, small marks of ownership, claiming him. "You forgive me, then?"

"Nothing to forgive. You belong with me. You belong with us. Jas..." His ass clenches, a spasm going through him, a breathless cry, and he's coming, shudders going through his strong frame as his cum splashes the wall. "Damn..."

I rock into him as deep as I can and hiss as my own orgasm hits. A tornado, a storm hurling me into the sky.

I'm not falling. I'm flying. For the first time in fucking ages, I'm alive.

My knees buckle and before I know it, we're both sliding

down to our knees on the wet floor. Peter is panting, and I think my heart might give out—but it would have been worth it.

Oh yeah, so worth it.

When I don't die and my lungs start working again, I kiss his neck. He harrumphs softly, turning his head to find my mouth.

The kiss is a whisper, a flicker, a seal of affection.

"Do you love me, Jas?" he asks.

I laugh helplessly. "Damn you, you know I fucking love you. Never stopped. Never will."

"Good," he says drowsily, his grin faint, grunting when I gently pull out of him. "Otherwise, tomorrow could be awkward. I'm not sure I can walk."

I laugh harder. "Want me to carry you around?"

"That's an idea. But what I meant is... fuck, I want you in my arms tonight. And tomorrow. And every day."

"That can be arranged."

"Damn, you..." He twists around, pulls me into his arms and I freeze. "How can I trust that this is real, that we can have this, after everything?"

Slowly I lift my arms and haul him against me. He's echoing my own thoughts. But... "Our doubts make it real."

He huffs a laugh. "Figured you'd have a weird answer to that."

I kiss his wet hair. "I do my best to entertain."

"Someone is knocking on the door," Peter says. "I swear for a hot moment I thought it was your watch."

"No. No more keeping time. We fulfilled our mission. Now it's time to live again."

He smiles, looks about to say something, when the door of the bathroom opens with a crash. His head jerks around. "What...?"

Everyone bursts in—Wendy, Tink, the Twins. Thankfully not her roommate.

"Are you guys okay?" Wes stalks over to us. "We couldn't find either of you and then we heard a noise, and... Oh."

"Oh?" Colt joins him and just stares at us where we're huddled, hugging on the shower stall floor. "Oh!"

"What's this about?" Wendy demands and shoves between them to see. "You guys... oh my God!"

"What?" I demand, starting to feel antsy. "Is there a problem?"

"With you guys fucking? None whatsoever," Colt says, a grin spreading on his face.

"Fucking?" Tink steps in front of Wes, hands on his hips, glaring. "Are you for real?"

I was fucking afraid of this. I take a breath to say something —we didn't clarify things with Tink before jumping into the shower, though in my defense I hadn't planned on sex—but Peter leans back and smiles at Tink.

"See? It worked out."

Tink shakes his head. "I wanted to see this!"

I blink. "You did?"

"The reunion of the two kings? Are you crazy? I demand a repeat."

"I second that," Wendy says, leaning her shoulder against Tink, a grin spreading on her face. "Guys?"

"We third and fourth that," the Twins say in one voice.

My mouth twitches. I'm at a loss for words, but the smiles on their faces tell me that everything is okay. Everything is fine.

And if doubting means this is real, then their reassurances make it even more so.

They have accepted me back into their circle, their group, into the family of all those who became lost and then were found.

25

WENDY

"Give me a bite of that. I'm starving." Wes tries to snatch the toast out of my hand and fails miserably.

"Oh, poor baby. Get your own." I take a big bite and chew, moaning a little at the taste. "So good..."

"Not fair, giving the toast a blowjob," Tink complains.

"That's cuz what you really want for breakfast is Wendy between your legs, blowing you," Wes says.

"Actually, I'd rather have her on the bed, underneath me," Tink says and winks at me.

That image... it lodges in my head and I forget to chew and swallow. "Um..."

"Maybe later," Wes says, "I'm hungry now." He makes another grab for my toast—and this time he gets it.

"Hey!" I start after him but he's too fast.

"Thievers keepers," he says with a grin and stuffs his mouth.

"That's not even a saying," I grumble. "Or a word."

"Mm, this is good." Wes winks at me, cheeks full like a squirrel. A blond, sexy squirrel...

Without a word, a crooked grin on his face, Colt passes me

his toast. I take a bite from it and glance around the kitchen table, smiling.

Wes is leaning against the counter, eating my stolen toast, looking proud of himself.

Peter is sitting on said counter, drinking his black coffee, trying to steal the toast from Wes with no success.

Jas is by the toaster, making a heap of toasts for everyone.

Tink is spreading butter and jam on them as they come out and passing them to Colt who is distributing them.

My boys.

I still can't believe they're here. Sometimes I get this feeling of disconnect when I watch them move about the apartment, because they're out of context, out of the world in which I met them.

Apart from Peter, of course. And Jas when he came to find me.

But those were brief encounters, and I didn't really know Peter when he saved me. Jas wasn't living here when I found him underneath my window.

Now this is their world.

They say they do want to stay. They say they are mortal, despite their twisted shadows.

I wonder if they will change, despite Peter's denials. If their shadows will heal. If they will become less violent.

I don't care. In bed, I hope they never change, and as for outside of sex, they are gentle with me and always have been. Their hearts are pure gold. I'm not afraid of the future.

"So what will you do?" Jas asks later, as we lounge on the sofa, all of us pressed together in a big heap. He strokes my hair and it feels so good. I think I might fall asleep right here.

"About what?"

"Your family," he says. "Won't you denounce what they did to you? Won't you go to the police?"

I frown. "No."

"Why not?"

"She just wants to live and be happy," Tink says, putting his arm around my shoulders. "Not drag this weight with her forever."

I shoot him a grateful look. "Yeah. That, exactly."

"And your brothers?" Peter asks.

"I am calling the police and social services," I whisper, resting my head on Colt's shoulder. "Today. Getting them out of there as quickly as possible, no matter what."

"Are you going to bring them here?" He glances around, a bit of doubt in his gaze. "Because..."

"The older one, Leonard, has turned eighteen and moving out next month. He wants John to stay with him. I have been saving money to bring them here to live with me, but..."

"But now there's no space in your bedroom?" Wes smirks.

I snort. "I was going to get a bigger place. But they want to live on their own. I think..." I sigh. "I think they don't feel so close to me anymore. Maybe they never have. I was always Dad's favorite, Mom's bad daughter, and then I left home the moment I could and never went back. I'm... scared."

"To face your parents?"

I nod. "I never spoke a word of what happened to anyone. When the police asked how I had fallen into the water, I said I slipped. Nobody ever suspected anything about my family. Who would have believed me? We always looked like a happy family to outsiders. But now..." I swallow hard. "Now I remember everything, I will file charges. Put them in jail. And yet the thought of them behind bars is somehow... disturbing."

"It's not an easy thing, doing what you are about to do," Colt says. "But it's the right thing. And you won't be alone. We will be with you."

I shoot him a grateful smile.

"As for your brothers, you could get reacquainted," Colt says softly. "I bet they love you. You're easy to love."

My face warms. "Thank you. Maybe. I hope to meet with them once they are out of that house. We'll go from there."

"Don't burn any bridges you can still mend," Jas says.

"So philosophical."

"It's the coffee and toast. It's the lightness of my heart." He smiles at me, and he seems calmer and... happy. Happier than I've ever seen him. "It's all of you."

"We'll get a bigger place," I tell them. "For us. The money I saved will come in handy."

"And we'll get jobs," Wes says, licking his fingers. "I'm sure there are things we can do."

"Like fight monsters and shoot game with our guns?" Colt mutters. "Maybe at the circus?"

"Shut up. We'll find something," Wes says. "Cheer up, man."

"And then we'll come home to you in the evenings," Peter says, "tired and sweaty, and fuck you on every surface of the house."

"Now that is so romantic," I mutter, grinning.

"If you wanted romantic," Peter says, "you wouldn't be with us."

"I think we're plenty romantic," Tink says.

"Preach, brother." Colt shoots him a smirk. "We're complex people."

"That we are," Peter agrees.

"You're perfect," I say. "Just the way you are."

That has them pressing in around me, their hands on my shoulders, my face, my neck, my hair.

"You saved the worlds," Peter says. "You saved us, too, saved us from death but also from ourselves. You faced your fears and made us face our feelings. We love you, Wendy Darling."

In my eyes, the air sparkles with stars and spangles as their power rises—mortals? I really don't think so. Once a god, always a god, the divine spark burning forever inside of them— and it caresses me everywhere. I'll always be their maiden, their

Persephone, and they'll always be my dark suitors, my treasured husbands.

"And you," I say, caressing their beloved faces, one by one, "have saved *me*, my loves. I am yours from now to forever."

"Second star to the right and straight on 'til morning."
— J.M. Barrie, Peter Pan

OTHER BOOKS FROM MONA BLACK!

Book 1 in the Cursed Fae Kings series (standalone fae romance novels series):

<u>The Merman King's Bride</u>

A cursed King of Faerie

A princess betrothed to a man she doesn't love

A kiss that will change everything

The last thing Princess Selina expects to find in the lake in the woods is a handsome merman. His name is Adar and he saves her, teases her, kisses her, and tells her she could break his curse.

Because, as it turns out, he's a Fae King, cursed to remain in merman form until he finds a princess to kiss him.

But one kiss is not enough and Selina has other problems.

Such getting engaged to a prince she isn't sure she even likes, let alone loves. Marrying him and having his children is not on her list of favorite things.

And now she's falling for the merman.

He's everything she could wish for in a man. Handsome, protective, kind. Except that he is Fae. And has a fishtail.

Still, she can't stop thinking about him. Keeps going back to him. Craves his kisses.

Would gladly have his babies.

Is this a spell, or is it love? Can she break the curse and save Adar? Will there be a happy ending to their story?

All a girl can do is try. After all, true love is worth fighting for and Selina knows she has found it.

This book is standalone novella-length NA romance fantasy novel, featuring mature situations with some dark themes and adult language. It is a retelling of the Frog Prince, with all the emotions, romance, spice and heat.

————

A completed Paranormal Reverse Harem series! Welcome to Pandemonium Academy!

<u>**"Of Boys and Beasts"**</u>

One's a werewolf with an ax to grind

Two's a vampire with a heart of coal

Three's a demon with a taste for pain

Four's a fae with a past of woe

Five's a girl who will take them down all

In revenge for the pain they've sown

So what if they're gorgeous? They must atone...

My name is Mia Solace. You know, the girl who will take them down all? That's me.

When my cousin is returned to us by Pandemonium Academy in a glass coffin, in an enchanted sleep she isn't expected to wake up from, I grab her diary and head to the academy myself.

Because her diary, you see, tells of four cruel boys who

bullied her and broke her heart until she sought oblivion through a spell.

Four magical boys, because that's the world we live in now, heirs of powerful families attending this elite academy where the privileged scions of the human and magical races are brought together in the noble pursuit of education.

As for me, I cheat to get on the student roster, and once I'm in, well... it's war, baby. I'll get those four sons of guns, steal their secrets, make them hurt. I'll transform into an avenging angel for my cousin, for all the girls they've wronged, and I bet there are plenty of those.

While growing up, my cousin was my only friend. Now I'll be her champion.

Only these boys aren't exactly as I pictured them. Devastatingly handsome, deliciously brooding, strangely haunted, they're getting under my skin and through my defenses.

Kissing them surely wasn't part of my plan...

Getting into bed with them even less.

ABOUT MONA BLACK

Mona is a changeling living in the human world. She writes fantasy romance and reverse harem romance, and is an avid reader of fantasy and paranormal books. One day she will get her ducks in a row and get a cat so she can become a real author.

Check out her paranormal reverse harem series Pandemonium Academy Royals, and her fantasy romance series Cursed Fae Kings.